*Pride Publishing books by Kegan Tyler*

**The Blood Crusades**
Blood Omen

# The Blood Crusades

# BLOOD OMEN

## KEGAN TYLER

Blood Omen
ISBN # 978-1-80250-953-3
©Copyright Kegan Tyler 2022
Cover Art by Kelly Martin ©Copyright May 2022
Interior text design by Claire Siemaszkiewicz
Pride Publishing

Published in 2022 by Pride Publishing, United Kingdom.

Pride Publishing is an imprint of Totally Entwined Group Limited.

# BLOOD OMEN

# Dedication

To Deena
for your endless love and support.

"Why be a wallflower when you can be a Venus fly trap?" ~ MARINA, *Venus Fly Trap*

# Author's Note

My character, Thomas, suffers from depression. But it's not just a fictional thing — depression is real, it affects us all to varying degrees throughout our lives and it is sinister. It can consume you and make life seem fruitless and empty.

To anyone out there dealing with mental illness, you are not alone. I struggle with Bipolar II disorder and an anxiety disorder. Every day, I face some level of depression, anxiety, mania or all of the above. But I persist.

And you will, too.

# Acknowledgements

This book would not have been made possible without the support of some very important people. First and foremost, thank you to my mother, Deena Cuda, for being my number one supporter. You've given me the confidence to be who I am, no matter what.

Thank you to Anna Olson, my editor. You helped me make this work as good as it could be and I am eternally grateful for that. And, of course, thank you for choosing my book.

Rebecca Scott, who aided me during the publishing process — thank you.

Thank you to Totally Entwined Group for providing great resources for getting started with publishing.

Thank you to Brooke Lauren, Jay Nate, Kelsey "Jelsew" Cook, Shane Coleman, Tyler Bottema, Joshua and Artie Alan, Debbie June, and Joe Michaletz for all of your support.

Thank you to my influences — Stephen King, for teaching me how to write great characters; Anne Rice, for giving me insight into building a rich and detailed world; and the Underworld films, for showing me how a real vampire-werewolf story is told. As well, thank you to the band Metric for giving me endless inspiration, and the UK artist MARINA, who inspired the epigraph.

Lastly, thank you to my readers for giving this book a chance. I spent eleven years developing this story, and you're the reason I created it.

# Prologue

In the Dark of Night

The lycan Rhyse Griesbach entered the apartment on a wet autumn night. The rain pecked against the glass door leading to the balcony just off the living area. The gleaming brilliance from the waxing moon cast a shadow of water droplets along the beige carpeting. A thundering boom from several miles away rattled the thin walls and sent a shiver down Rhyse's spine. It was colder than it should have been on a rainy fall evening in Creston Bay, Wisconsin.

He stepped forward cautiously, aware of the smells in this modest living space, kept relatively tidy except for a few dirty dishes on the coffee table in front of him. Those must have been there longer than a day — the smell of old, room-temperature Chinese takeout filled his sensitive nostrils, and he cringed away, reaching for the door to the balcony.

The door was aged and rickety, and its tracks hadn't been oiled in a very long time, as was evident by the screech it made as he swung the heavy slab of glass to the side. Somehow, Mother Earth's mystical forces made the storm worse than it had been – the rain came zipping down sideways, slamming against the hard rubber of his trench coat. He flicked his collar up, though it wouldn't do much more to protect him from getting wet. He didn't mind getting soaked... The rain, when gentle, relaxed him, made him feel at one with his surroundings and cleared his head. But this rain... This storm was angry.

He arched his neck upward, his wet brown hair sticking to his forehead, and bared his sharp canines as he sniffed the air. Several stories below, just across the street, a line of moviegoers piled in under the Bay Theater marquee, waiting to get their tickets for the first showing of *Nightstalkers IV: Awakening*. From the fourth floor of the apartment building, Rhyse could smell the hot blood coursing through the veins of each person below him, could smell their fear.

*Fear... Too much fear in the world now...*

Then, in a stroke of pure irony, he sensed movement behind him, from inside the apartment. He whipped his head around, peering through the glass, his glowing orange irises reflecting back at him. His lycan eyes showed him nothing – which wasn't good at all. It meant that something inhuman was watching him.

The Nightstalker came into view just before she smashed herself through the door, its glass sending shards in every direction. Rhyse faced the theater again and leapt in the air above the bustling street of the downtown district. He heard the Nightstalker hiss behind him as she, too, dove into empty space in pursuit.

Rhyse landed on the marquee just above the ticket station. From below, one of the humans in line screamed and pointed from under her bubblegum-pink umbrella. "It's one of them!"

Rhyse growled at her, a throaty, preternatural sound that carried through the streets. Then he grabbed hold of a large vertical light decoration—a staple of the theater chain—that alternated in colorful patterns of blues, pinks, yellows and purples. He reached the top of the spire and grabbed hold of the ledge of the rooftop. He swung himself up and landed quick on his heels, darting toward the adjacent building.

The Nightstalker wasn't far behind. She carried a grappling hook with her and used it to hoist herself up the side of the building. Rhyse was almost to the opposite edge of the theater when she aimed and shot her hook at his feet. Its sharp end twisted in mid-air, heading straight toward Rhyse's ankles. Then, just as he leapt into the air, the pointed edge of the tool sliced through his Achilles' tendon and jutted out the other side, its sharp hooks expanding and clenching around his ankle. Fresh blood sprayed on the concrete, and he fell on his chest, his temple slamming into the ledge. His surroundings began to spin, and black spots danced around his field of vision.

The Nightstalker reeled him in and he yelped from the pain as the thick wire attached to the hook pulled Rhyse toward her. She pressed a button on the side of her weapon which released the wire from the hook. The wire zipped back into the gun-shaped device. Then she perched on the balls of her feet beside him.

Rhyse looked up and, as his vision steadied and the pain began to subside, the Nightstalker's silhouette eclipsed the bright yellow moon in the clouded sky. She snarled at him with predatory white teeth and a black tongue that slithered between them as she hissed, a revolting sound not unlike a cat's as it prepared to pounce.

She gripped the hook lodged in Rhyse's ankle and tugged on it, releasing it from the bloodied wound which was desperately trying to heal itself.

"Listen to me closely," she said, her words slimy and condemning. "Tell your leader we're watching. We see your hideout on the lake and we know where you live. We will reign, and if your pack is so naïve as to pursue us, we will exterminate you. We are more powerful than your precious André can imagine, and there are many more of us than you believe.

"Abandon your efforts or die," she delivered as a final, malevolent threat, and stood upright. She removed something concealed within her raincoat pocket and dropped it on his chest. It was a silver cross with a figure of Jesus nailed to it.

The weight of a thousand pounds fell on his torso and he couldn't breathe. The blood pumping through his veins grew louder, thunk-thunking in his head. He reached a shaking hand to the cross and braced himself for the heat. Then he gripped it in his palm, screamed as it seared his skin, and threw it aside. It clanked against the concrete—a sound more piercing than the Nightstalker's ungodly hiss.

The weight lifted, and he sucked in a deep breath. He stayed there on the rooftop for a while, staring up at the gray clouds as the rain ceased.

# Chapter One

Shift

Thomas Allen Wright ascended the steps to the front entrance of his apartment building, sopping wet from the relentless rain and craving a cocktail. He realized as he entered the passcode into the security pad that he'd be walking into an empty apartment, and he would spend the night alone for the first time in a week.

His ongoing affair with Jonathan Greer, a corporate snooze with money and a raucous lifestyle, had come to a screeching halt as of late. For a long while, Jonathan had stayed with Thomas in his apartment, and was always there after Thomas' late shift at the café. Thomas reminisced fondly about the countless nights they'd shared in each other's company, all the hot lovemaking they'd indulged in. Jonathan liked to call it 'fucking' as he was still putting up a straight-acting façade for his black-tie boys in the office, which, much to Thomas' discomfort, translated into Jonathan's day-to-day life as well. And, somehow, it translated to the bedroom.

But perhaps that was why Thomas had been so drawn to him. Jonathan's macho disposition coupled with his impossibly sculpted tan body made him irresistible. So much so that Thomas had found himself in the most ridiculous situations to be at Jonathan's beck and call. He was too devoted, and for what? A good lay?

All this swirled in his head as he progressed down the hallway and to the elevator at the far end of the building. He slapped the *Up* button and waited for it to descend. He set his briefcase down on the checker-patterned carpet and ran his fingers through his dark brown hair, wringing out the excess water dribbling down his leather jacket.

Thomas knew deep down that he was an attractive man with his cerulean eyes and timid smile. But he didn't believe it himself. He'd often stare at his feet when good-looking men walked past him, or when girls smiled and winked at him on the street.

Like his mane of brown hair, his loafers were unkempt — scuffed, scratched and faded — and their age clearly showed. He looked about thirty, but he never disclosed his real age to anyone, not even his closest lover.

He was a shapeshifter. The animal he transformed into most commonly was a wolf, though he could take on many forms at any given moment. He'd once been a panther, which was his second-favorite creature to shift into. He so often chose a werewolf for the obvious reason — if anyone in the area were to see him in his animal form, he'd not be blinked at more than twice. Werewolves were accepted as part of society now, no longer a myth. If anyone had come across him as a panther, he'd be on the local news and, more than likely, a hunt would be called. How unusual it would be to see an exotic animal that was most prominent in the jungle in the Great Lakes. Lycans had been 'out' to the world for about ten years at this point, so he figured he'd blend in posing as one.

Perhaps the most useful part of his unique gift was the ability to not just shift into an animal but to shift into another person. He had first discovered this when he was twelve, in the bathroom stall of his middle school. A bully, whose name he'd long since forgotten, had maneuvered him into the girls' room and was taunting him, shouting obscenities at the top of his lungs and banging on the stall door with his meaty fists. Desperate for an escape, little Thomas had shifted into Becca, a classmate he was friends with, and pranced out of the girls' room, laughing under his breath at the look on his bully's face when she exited the stall instead of him.

This became a fun little game in his youth, and it had expanded in adulthood. By now he'd adopted the appearances of some ten or eleven figures, a couple of them celebrities, and he had found it amusing to trick and confuse those around him. He quite enjoyed living someone else's life now and then.

The result of this special ability was that he had an alter ego. Evan Winston was his name, and he was a British scholar from Edinburgh on visa in the United States to study biology at the University of Wisconsin in Oshkosh. Or so he told people. A completely fictional character with an appearance Thomas had appropriated from a fashion model in the UK, Evan was blond-haired, blue-eyed, and had a nice large cock which was useful in bed. Thomas' own was a bit smaller with a modest girth, and this, paired with his prominent ass, meant that he bottomed all the time...in his true form. As Evan, he enjoyed the pleasure of being on top *and* having a sizable eight-inch cock. What a dream it was to be Mr. Evan Winston.

Jonathan did not know Evan, and Thomas intended to keep it that way. As a personal rule, he never used his trickery on those closest to him. Presently, the two people that met that criterion were Jonathan and his best friend Shalese.

One other secret that Thomas carried with himself was that he could never visibly age past where he was. His real age was sixty-two, though every time he shifted back to himself, he looked about thirty. He had the most coveted ability in all human existence — immortality, or at least that's what he considered it. He had the pleasure of watching the world evolve around him, passing through multiple generations while maintaining an appearance much younger than all he interacted with. He'd see friends age and once they noticed that he looked the same as he did when they first met him, it was time to pack up his life and relocate. He'd traveled from New York City, where he was born, to Sacramento and all places in between. For a brief time, he'd lived on the Mediterranean coast, but had decided that the community was too closely knit. Others looked at him with suspicion, and he suspected that several of the city residents knew what he was. He had lasted five months there.

When Thomas touched a living being, the DNA of that life form would transfer to him, and his body would keep a record of that form at that point in time — the age, the shape... Everything about that being as it was when he touched it, he would transform into. He could shift into a variety of life forms, such as a snake, a dove and a Northern cardinal.

He'd never forget the time he met his childhood crush, Ava Charlotte, in person. A superstar pop icon, she had been much more reserved and humble than he'd imagined. He'd shaken her hand, and she'd given him the warmest smile in passing. She was thirty-four at the time, so whenever he shifted, she looked the same as she was that day. He carried the memory with him fondly and would shift into her physique every now and then to remember it.

He'd seen all kinds of men from all parts of the United States, and he'd gotten pretty good at guessing what their cocks looked like. He estimated he'd slept with close to seven hundred men throughout the country. His favorite were the solid boys with a southern drawl and an appetite for ass. They always had the nicest cocks. It was the Jersey boys and the surfers that had the most obnoxious personalities, and the smallest penises.

Thomas reached his apartment door and dug into his pocket for his keys, brushing against the head of his half-hard cock. He fumbled for the right key and, as he slid it in, it reminded him of the times he'd don Evan Winston and slide into those beautiful country boys. He overheard a conversation between a police officer, Thomas' landlord and the tenant of apartment five. The man was irate, shouting something about an intruder shattering his balcony door. The officer asked if anything was stolen, to which the man said no, not that he could see. The landlord muttered a comment about not paying for the damages. When the man's voice raised an octave, Thomas took that as his cue to hide.

He flung the door open and closed it behind him, then shed his clothes, tossing them to the floor. He slumped down onto the black sofa and played with himself, fantasizing about Jonathan and the way he so expertly made Thomas come while giving him oral.

Thomas was aware of the fact that he lived in Jonathan's shadow, and no amount of pity or self-reliance could change that. His mind was always glued to Jonathan's body, to his full, pink lips, to his sizable prospect too often concealed behind slim jeans. When he came on himself, he ran his fingers through the fresh hot cum and imagined Jonathan's sensual hands sliding along his torso. Then he envisioned Jonathan spreading his ass and nuzzling his crevice into Thomas' face. As he fantasized about licking Jonathan's tight hole, his eager hand traced his abdomen and reached for his cock again, working it until he came a second time.

In a daze, he rolled off the couch and grabbed his nearby shirt, using it to clean himself off. Then he grabbed his other forgotten clothes and stashed them in his laundry basket just inside the bedroom. He dipped into the bathroom and indulged in a hot shower, all the while letting Jonathan's hypnotic trance take over him.

After he'd stepped out of the shower and dried off, he wrapped the damp towel around his waist then reached into the pocket of his jeans in the basket for his phone. He looked up Jonathan's contact and dialed.

Four rings later, he was greeted with a melancholy woman. *"Your call has been forwarded to an automated voice message system..."* He pressed the *End* button and tossed the phone onto his bed in a mild fit of annoyance. Of course, whenever *he* wanted to get ahold of Jonathan, he was never available. But the second

Jonathan wanted to get ahold of him, Thomas answered at the first ring.

He knew he was too tied up in this delusion that he and Jonathan were meant to be, or rather that they were *good together*, which in itself was a fallacy. He knew for a fact that Jonathan couldn't give a damn about him and what he spent his time doing. He guessed that if Jonathan knew that he thought of him so often, he'd probably either shrug it off or ditch him altogether. This thought ravaged Thomas' mind as he made himself a vegetable stir-fry.

As he was about to dish up the food, his cell phone rang. Eagerly, he bolted into the bedroom and answered. The rough, sexy voice on the other end was unmistakable.

"What's up?"

"Hey, Jonathan," Thomas said with a sigh. "What are you doing tonight?"

"I just got back from a twelve-hour day," Jonathan grumbled. He sounded worn. "Mounds of paperwork and bitchy clients. My head fuckin' hurts."

"I bet it does," Thomas sympathized. Then, feeling ballsy, he said, "Would a blow job help?"

Jonathan sighed, and there was a brief pause. Then he said, "Yeah, it would. I've been thinking about your ass all day. I want it."

"Come over. I'm making stir-fry."

Another sigh. "I can't drive."

"Why is that?"

"I'm a little drunk," Jonathan confessed.

"Already? When did you get home?"

"Yeah, already. About an hour ago. Downed five shots and I'm on my second beer."

"How about I bring the food over to you?"

"Mmmmh," Jonathan moaned. Thomas imagined he was biting his lip. "Sex *and* free food. Sign me up."

"I can be there in twenty."

"Make it fifteen." *Click.*

\* \* \* \*

Thomas made it fifteen.

Or seventeen, to be precise. He pulled into the driveway of Jonathan's condominium. His dashboard read 11:01 p.m. He yawned and slid out of his car. The chilling autumn air nipped at his nose, crystallizing his breath. He locked the car before walking up the steps to Jonathan's front door, then knocked, standing around while hugging his arms. The container of hot food warmed his palm.

Jonathan answered a moment later. His eyes were glazed over, and he was clearly *drunk*-drunk. He reeked of cinnamon whiskey.

"C'mere, sexy," he mumbled, tugging at Thomas' pants and guiding him inside. He greeted him with a wet kiss on the mouth, and four more on his neck.

"Food first?" Thomas asked.

Jonathan looked at him like he was delusional. "No. I want your ass first."

Thomas dropped the container and shuffled over to the huge tan couch against the far wall of Jonathan's living room. All the lights were off, save for a night light in the bathroom, which was bright enough to highlight Jonathan's insatiable torso as he whipped his shirt over his head and flung it aside.

The moonlight leaked in from the west through the bay window. The curtains were wide open, but Thomas didn't care. His body was writhing with anticipation.

The silver light from the moon danced across Jonathan's abdomen, showcasing all the curves of his muscles and the deep crevice in the middle of his chest. He was already breathing quite heavily — he, too, writhed with desire. His pecs moved inward and out, and his large brown nipples were rock-solid. His short-cropped black hair was awry, and his brown eyes looked down on Thomas' body as he slipped out of his clothes.

As Thomas gripped the band of his tight black underwear, Jonathan grabbed his hands and said, "No, this is my favorite part."

Thomas let his arms fall to his sides, and Jonathan glided his hands up and down his abdomen, feeling every rivet of his muscles. Then Jonathan nibbled at the pulsating bulge concealed behind the designer underwear. Jonathan reached up into Thomas' crotch through his underwear and let loose his hard cock. He sensually licked the head, and it jumped in response. Then he wrapped his lips around it and gave it a suck. Thomas bit his lip and moaned.

Then, off came the underwear. They slipped down his legs like silk and hung around his ankles as Jonathan gripped his shaft in a fist and sucked on Thomas' balls. Thomas inhaled. Jonathan let go and slid his lips down the shaft of Thomas' cock. A wave of ecstasy overcame Thomas as Jonathan sucked on his dick, keeping it pulsing in his mouth for a second, then he sucked in a breath and released. Thomas' cock slapped against his own stomach, Jonathan's wet saliva sticking to his skin.

Jonathan grabbed him by the waist and flipped him over. Thomas rested his arms on the top of the couch and spread his legs.

Jonathan slapped his ass cheeks, making a satisfying *smack* reverberate throughout the room. Thomas groaned. Jonathan dove right in, nuzzled his face in Thomas' furry crevice and playfully licked his hole. Thomas took a sharp inhalation, arching his back, his muscles constricting. Jonathan's nose brushed against the hairs on his ass, and he closed his eyes as Jonathan slithered his tongue into Thomas' hole, wetting it for what was coming next.

After a few breaths of air and several minutes of rimming, Jonathan pulled away.

Then, Thomas gasped as he felt his lover enter him from behind, Jonathan's sizable cock sliding deep into his body. The first thrust was always the most painful. His muscles contracted around Jonathan's cock. Jonathan pulled out and went back in all the way this time, pushing until his balls touched Thomas'. Jonathan gained momentum, gripping Thomas' hips and pulling him in as he pounded him. Thomas let out a short gasp every time Jonathan's cock hit the deepest point.

Thomas closed his eyes, gathering his breath and preparing for the next thrust. The initial pain was over. Now he could indulge in the pleasure of his lover inside him.

\* \* \* \*

An hour later, while Jonathan snored on his shoulder, Thomas stared out of the window into the night sky — at the moon. Its brilliance shone down upon him as it whispered the sweet, sweet song of power, of transformation in his ear. He closed his eyes and listened, his inner animal fighting to get out. His teeth sharpened. His blood thickened, and it ran vigorously through his veins.

He opened his eyes and slid out from Jonathan's lazy grasp. He gathered his clothes, bunched them up, then snuck out of the front door.

The night welcomed him. It beckoned him into the darkness, into the gaze of the pale moon above, the powerful entity that controlled the tides of Lake Angular, that whisked him away into an unrelenting night, where he was free. Free to run, to roar, to howl. The moon was his goddess, the light that shone the way through the darkness of the forest beyond the lake.

He ducked out into the chilly evening naked, with his clothes bundled up in front of his groin. He unlocked his car and tossed them on the passenger seat, then slammed it shut, locked it, and flung the keys into a bush under Jonathan's bay window.

Then he shifted.

The ripples began at the core of his chest, where his heart thudded beneath his ribs. They ebbed through his body, rushing through his skin like waves on the sand. Blood raced through his veins as they grew and thickened. His muscles burned as they expanded and his bones ached. His teeth became razor-sharp, and his nose and mouth elongated into a pronounced muzzle. Thick brown fur burst from the pores on his skin, and pleasure rocked his core. His dick hardened, nestling itself in his pubic hair as that, too, became fur.

He held back the urge to howl until he reached the other side of the lake. For now, a low grumble would do.

He set off down the street toward the bridge that crossed Lake Angular, connecting the peninsula of Creston Bay to Moore's Island on the other side. He noted how magnificent the trees looked, how the moonlight glided across the windswept branches and treetops.

There were no cars on the road, which was just as well. Thomas leapt over the bridge to the island and raced through the trees. He mounted a boulder among a large set of stones in a clearing. Then he arched his back and howled at the sky, letting the power of the moon consume him.

The nocturnal creatures of the forest felt his influence, and they scattered into the thick branches. He heard them scurry and pursued them.

Then, far in the distance, he heard a howl.

He stood upright and sniffed the air. His powerful senses detected another predator deep within the bowels of the forest. His heart thudded in its enlarged cavity, and with a grumble, he darted through the woods.

As he grew closer, the creature's pulse resounded in Thomas' head.

It was expecting him.

Up ahead, the moonlight shined down through the trees into a clearing of long grass. He slowed to a crawl, peering about for the creature.

Then he saw it.

Standing on all fours about a foot higher than Thomas, another werewolf loomed across the clearing. The glistening moonlight shimmered across its beautiful, thick coat of black fur. Its eyes stood out against the dark backdrop—they glowed a brilliant crimson. The lycan growled, a foreign sound so deep that Thomas was struck with amazement.

*This is an alpha wolf.*

Thomas stepped forward into the clearing, and his brown fur looked almost red in the pale moonlight. The other wolf grumbled, and saliva dripped from its teeth. Thomas heard its voice inside his head.

*"Shift,"* it said.

Thomas had an overwhelming urge to obey and reluctantly shifted into Evan Winston, naked and exposed. His pasty complexion looked even more so in the unrelenting white light from above. Goosebumps rose on his skin, and he hugged his arms, shivering.

Slowly, the alpha wolf sauntered toward him, and it snarled in his face once it was close enough. Though its beauty was striking, Evan cringed at its breath, hot and wet in his face. It looked like it was going to eat him or injure him and leave him to die.

But then, something changed in its eyes, and suddenly the wolf was gone.

In its place was a nude man, as beautiful as his animal. He looked down at Evan, who had fallen to his knees, his waist tickled by the tendrils of grass swaying in the breeze. The man was a feat of wonder, with a mighty, barbarian frame and long black hair that grazed his nipples, hard from the evening chill. His chest jutted out several inches from his abdomen, with pecs so bulbous they looked about to burst. His arms were the size of cannons, and his lower abdomen was coated in black hair, which led to his frighteningly massive cock dangling at Evan's eye level. It hung over a pair of testicles the size of tennis balls, all nestled in the crevice of his muscled thighs.

Evan studied the man's face. Strong, masculine, and daring, the man's hard angled features defined his aura. He scowled at Evan from above, his thick eyebrows bunched close together. His lips curled in a sneer.

"What is your name?" the man said. His voice poured from his mouth like velvet.

"Evan," he said, standing up.

"How long have you been here?"

Evan gave him a puzzled look. "I've been in the area for a while."

"And have you ever wandered to these parts before tonight?"

He nodded. "Yes, indeed. I come here often to hunt prey and run with my wolf."

"I've not sensed you here before," the man said, looking Evan up and down, seeming to pause for a moment on his dick, shriveled by the cold.

"Well, I rarely venture this deep into the forest."

"Why come to these parts?"

"These parts?" Evan said with curiosity. "What's so special about them? It's just a forest. A rather nice one at that."

"This territory belongs to the Bramwell pack." It was stated matter-of-factly. "You are trespassing."

Evan took a step forward. The man glanced at his feet as he did. Then, Evan said, "On whose property?"

The man inched closer as well, baring his teeth, and snarled, "Mine."

Evan glared at him, balling his fists and preparing for a fight.

"Don't be a fool," the man said through gritted teeth. "Back off. It is not your place."

"Who are you to me?" Evan dared to ask.

"I am André Mandelar, alpha leader of the Bramwell pack of the Great Lakes," he growled. "This is our territory, as has been claimed for centuries."

"Then why does Highway 41 run through it?"

André glared at him and looked about to say something. Then Evan noticed something change in his demeanor.

"You're not a lycanthrope," André whispered.

"Beg pardon?"

"You are not a lycan," André repeated. "You are something else. What are you?"

"I—I'm not—"

"Show me what you are," André commanded.

Evan could have explained to this man that he was simply a werewolf, nothing more—but his fear bested him, so again he obeyed, shifting back into his natural form.

"Incredible," André gasped.

"You think so?" Thomas said.

"Yes, very much so," the man responded. "I've never seen anything like it in a thousand years."

"Damn. You have me beat, old man. I've lived for sixty-two years."

"You...you are a gifted one. You're what they call a—*shapeshifter*."

"Wait," Thomas said. "You've lived a thousand years and not once met a shapeshifter?"

"No, never," he answered. "Your kind are *extremely* rare."

"You can't be serious," Thomas scoffed. "Nothing's special about me."

"On the contrary, my friend," he said, "you are the most special person I've ever met... Would you like to join my pack?"

Thomas was caught off guard. "Join your pack?"

"Yes. We could use someone as gifted as you. And now has never been a more crucial point in history for a strong alliance."

"I dunno," Thomas said. "Packing up all my shit and sharing a house in the woods with a crowd of man-wolves seems just a tad desperate. No offense. Besides, I've always been alone. I'm good at it. I don't do well in groups."

"From what I've learned, no shapeshifter does," André said.

Thomas gave him an inquisitive look. He stepped closer. "What else do you know about shapeshifters?"

"I've learned very little over the centuries," he confessed. "But what knowledge I do possess of your kind, however limited, is invaluable."

"I didn't even know others like me existed," Thomas said, looking down at his bare feet.

"Oh, dear boy, of *course* others like you exist."

Thomas thought for a moment. Then, he said, "If I did join your little...erm, *pack*, would you teach me?"

"Teach you about shapeshifters?"

Thomas nodded.

André shrugged and said, "Certainly. As I said, we'd be honored to have you."

Thomas wanted to follow André back to wherever his pack lived but couldn't bring himself to the idea of sharing a space with others. And, truthfully, it unnerved him to think of being taken away from Jonathan, even if he couldn't give Thomas more than an hour of attention.

But the desire to know more about his origin burned like a wildfire inside him. He yearned for solitude, but he ached to know others like him, to feel like he was not alone on this forsaken planet.

"May I come back?" Thomas asked.

"Of course," André answered. "Any time you're ready, we'll be here. I presume you know of the castle by the shore?"

"The long-abandoned castle some ritzy couple in De Pere inherited? Get the fuck out of town. You don't *live* there!"

André chuckled. "Yes, we do. And we'd like to keep up the illusion that the castle is vacant, so spare yourself the trouble of bragging about tonight."

"Who's gonna believe me?" Thomas cackled. "This is fucking crazy. You live in a goddamned *castle*. For fuck's sake…"

"Well, I hope that doesn't change your mind," André said.

Thomas chuckled to himself and rubbed his eyes. "It's late. I need to get back home. I'll…think about it."

"Please do," André said. "We'd be willing to accommodate your stay to make it more comfortable for you in any way."

"Sure," Thomas said with a wave. "Nice meeting you."

"It was an honor, Evan," André replied with a nod.

"Thomas," he said with a small smile. "My name is Thomas." He turned his back to the man and shifted once more into his wolf. He ran through the woods, over the bridge, and shifted back into himself as he approached his car in front of Jonathan's condo. He reached in the brush under the window for his keys and, upon finding them, unlocked the door to his car.

Quickly, he threw on his clothes then climbed in the driver's side. He started the car and, shivering, warmed his fingers by the vent as lukewarm heat came through.

He drove home alone without a longing glance behind him as he left Jonathan's home, which he'd always done before. But not this time.

*Not this time.*

# Chapter Two

## Transformation

Thomas arrived home around four a.m. He stumbled through his dark apartment in a haze. It was ethereal and intoxicating. He'd never felt so relieved in his life. Finally, after sixty-two years of searching, he'd found out there were others like him. Seclusion was his specialty, and it couldn't be mere coincidence that he'd been led to the Bramwell pack that night.

As elated as he was, his body was weak with exhaustion, and his bed called to him. He didn't bother flicking any light switches. He landed on his bed with a *thunk*.

His mind ebbed into unconsciousness and a horrifying vision replaced reality.

*Thomas was standing on the edge of a cliff. The chilling night winds didn't make him shudder – it was the sky. It wasn't just black... It was a void. The cliff descended into darkness, and the craggy rocks he stood upon trembled. He turned around and cringed at the sight before him.*

*A vast landscape of decrepit, ancient buildings – what once was brown stucco was now a pile of crumbling rocks.*

An old fountain in the heart of the city was carved into the earth, but all remnants of water were dried up. Its alabaster was lifeless, devoid of shine. Dirt filled the cracks in the stone, and the metal spout was warped by eons of rust. The fountain, cracked in half at jagged ends, sunk into a massive pit that was once the central square. It remained erect at a forty-five-degree angle, casting a looming shadow over the rocks around it.

Death was here.

The cries of a thousand tortured souls, trapped here in a void where life could no longer exist, resounded throughout the square. A fallen city on a massive rock suspended in a sea of endless black.

An old relic materialized within reach – a porcelain doll with no eyes and half a jaw. Its hair had been singed off by a ravaging fire. Its hollow eyes stared at him without context – empty, faceless vessels. It wore a charred, blackened dress and was missing a shoe. Its arm was extended out to Thomas, as though it were pleading with him.

A woman's piercing shriek rang through his ears. "My baby!" she cried, a wailing banshee in the wind.

Her cries grew stronger, and Thomas' knees began to quiver. He fell to the dust and gripped the sides of his head, clenching his teeth and squeezing his eyes shut as her screams echoed.

"Please, someone – my baby – please!"

He heard a scuffle and felt dirt on his face. He opened his eyes – the doll was standing upright in front of him. Startled, he jumped back. His arms fell behind him to break the fall. The doll stared him down with those menacing black holes, ripping him apart from the inside.

Its head twisted sharply to the right. The sound of scraping porcelain made his eardrums bleed and sent tremors raging through his muscles. It floated toward him, and he scrambled back, desperate to escape its glare.

*A dirty, leathery hand gripped his arm. He turned and gasped in horror at a withered corpse looking at him. It, too, had no eyes — just dried, hollow sockets. It cried out in pain and croaked, "My baby! Help, my baby!" A thick, yellow worm slithered out of the corner of its mouth.*

*He screamed and ripped his arm from the corpse's grip. He scrambled to his feet and ran. His vision was blurred from hot tears and the skin where the corpse had touched him began to burn and itch.*

*He tripped and landed his knee on a shard of glass. His face planted into the dirt, and he howled in agony. Sharp pain jutted up his side. He could not move.*

*The corpse crawled toward him. The sound of rotted flesh scraping against dirt made him retch. A gray hand slapped his pool of vomit, spraying chunks against his face. The corpse pulled itself up to his head and touched his cheek. He felt another worm slither through its fingers and onto his neck. The hand grasped his jaw and propped his mouth open. The corpse leaned into him, and he screamed.*

\* \* \* \*

Thomas woke instantly. He jumped out of his bed and ran his fingers all over himself. He could still feel the worm on his neck, the hot vomit on his cheek, could still smell the putrid, rotting corpse. He took a few deep breaths and felt his way in the dark to the bathroom. *What the hell was that? The end of the world?*

He flicked on the light, a dull fluorescent white with a bluish hue that made all the stains and grime stand out against the whitewash. He looked at his reflection in the mirror. He was dripping with sweat.

His heart was pounding in his chest, a constant *thu-thunk-thu-thunk-thu-thunk*. In the mirror, a hard-faced young man stared back at him. Thin, short-cropped brown hair, a chiseled jawline, and effervescent blue eyes scowled at him. The tattoo on his chest — a single red rose, inspired by his late mother — was partly concealed by chest hair. This was his true self — the appearance he'd come to know.

But Thomas lacked the confidence of a shapeshifter — a type of confidence he imagined one like him would have. He was deeply insecure, and underneath it all, what he wanted most was to belong.

His shabby apartment had become his safe zone. A four-hundred-square-foot box with a living room, kitchen, dining room and bedroom squished into a singular rectangle was all he'd ever wanted when he'd moved to Creston Bay fifteen years ago. Back then, as muscular and messy as ever, he had looked the same. In fact, he caught a wave of déjà vu from staring at his reflection. He might as well have been staring at a photograph. Nothing in this apartment had changed in those fifteen years, and because he always submitted his checks to the landlord on time every month and was never home for inspections, no questions were asked. For all his landlord knew, he was in his mid-forties.

He checked the time. It was eight a.m. on Sunday, and he didn't have to work. He decided he'd spend the day inside — give himself some time to mull over joining the pack. *Shalese could help, too.*

He reached for his phone and called his best friend. She picked up after the third ring.

"Hey doll, what's up?" Shalese said.

"I've got something to run by you," Thomas said. He was hesitant to tell her — after all, she'd be the first person ever to know he had supernatural abilities — but he went on. "I'm, uh...part...lycan."

Silence. And then —

"That's fucking awesome!"

"You think so? I mean, you're not freaked out by it?"

"No, not at all," she replied. "I think lycans are cool. Vampires, too. I always knew they were real."

Thomas chuckled. "You did. I remember when they first were discovered, you had a celebration. What did you call it—Vampire Pride Day?" They laughed at the memory.

"So that's why you've always looked so youthful," Shalese said.

"I guess so, yeah. Anyway, now, for what I need to ask. And I'm not supposed to be telling anyone about this so it has to stay between us, okay?"

"Yes, totally, I promise."

"All right. Last night I went out for a run through Moore's Forest and came across an alpha wolf—the leader of this pack of lycans that live in that old castle."

"No way," she whispered.

"And they want me to move in with them."

"Really? Why?"

Thomas bit his lip. He hadn't thought of what he'd tell her in this instance. He couldn't give away his secret—a half-truth about being a lycan, sure—but he needed to keep his shapeshifting powers to himself. "They just like me. I don't know."

"Hmm. Well, I think that's dope as hell. So what do you need to run by me?" Shalese asked.

"Whether I should do it."

"Thomas! Of course you should do it! You always talk about how you have no other friends and I think it would be healthy for you. Plus, you hate that apartment."

"I do not, I love this place."

"Yeah, right. It's tiny, Tom. Itty bitty. Not even a worm would be comfortable in there. Go live in that castle, okay? And send me pictures of the inside because I've always wondered what it looks like."

"Sure thing, Shalese. Thanks for your advice. I'll think about it."

"Of course, darling," she said. "See you at work tomorrow."

They said goodbye and Thomas ended the call.

He'd spent fifteen monotonous years in this small apartment, night after night alone with a twenty-inch set top box and an original PlayStation, then later, an Xbox 360 and a slowly growing collection of DVDs. Now he had a modest thirty-two-inch TV and a PlayStation 4, with maybe two or three Blu-rays. It was all he needed, and all he wanted. It was just him, his tiny media collection, and his browser history of porn. Occasionally, Jonathan would stay in his apartment and tease him for not upgrading to a 4K television while they watched Pornhub, and Thomas sucked Jonathan's dick.

*Fucking Jonathan. What a waste of time that man is. I don't need him.*

And he didn't—not for the number of times he'd offered his loyalty to this man, this self-centered egomaniac with a muscular body and a beautiful dick. Not for the countless nights he spent wondering what Jonathan was doing, and why he wasn't responding to his text messages, or answering his calls. Nor for the constant devotion Thomas showed him whenever he, Jonathan, wanted to get off or have his ass eaten or get his dick sucked while he lounged on the couch and watched videos of other hotter people fucking. No, it was a huge waste of time, and he and Jonathan had been hooking up on average once a week for ten years. All the while, Jonathan aged and developed crow's feet and his gorgeous mane of jet-black hair sprinkled with fine lines of silver, but Thomas looked just as he had been when they'd first met. But Jonathan had never noticed, nor cared. *He prefers instead to watch hot men pound each other on a flatscreen while I suck him off, not once paying attention to my body, or my ass that constricts back to virgin tightness when I shift. What a waste of ten years...*

These dizzying thoughts swirled around in his head, and he dozed off as he contemplated breaking it off with Jonathan.

\* \* \* \*

He awoke as he got a call. He checked the time again—ten p.m. He'd slept the entire day away. Groggily, he answered.

"Hullo?"

"Hey."

It was Jonathan.

"Hey," Thomas said back. There was a short pause. Then a sniffle. Jonathan was crying. "Everything all right?" he asked.

"Yeah. Yeah, I'm fine. It's just work and deadlines and..." Another sniffle. "You know, I could really use a buddy right now."

*A buddy. What?*

"You mean a fuck buddy."

"No, Thomas, I mean...it would be nice, but...I just want someone to hold right now."

This struck something within Thomas and suddenly, he felt bad about having those thoughts about Jonathan earlier.

"Hey," he said, "don't worry. I'm on my way."

\* \* \* \*

Thomas thought long and hard on the drive to Jonathan's condo. He decided he needed to leave his wretched day job at that call center and the night shift at the café. He needed to belong to something. And he had a feeling that was exactly what André's pack would offer him.

Fifteen years, and this was the life he had made for himself in such a beautiful city, this whole time with a pack of lycans, creatures with abilities similar to his own, living in a castle just across the bridge. He was so frustrated with himself he could scream.

A thought occurred to him just then. Maybe he'd stop somewhere on the way and get Jonathan something to cheer him up. He swung by Devin's, a breakfast joint with world-famous pies. He asked the cashier for a slice of blackberry pie, and she packaged it up for him, rang him up, and he was out of there in minutes. The diner was completely dead, which it ought to be at ten o'clock.

*Easy run.*

He pulled into Jonathan's driveway three minutes later. He walked up to the door, gave it a gentle knock, then opened it.

"Jonathan?" he said.

"Up here," Jonathan shouted from his bedroom upstairs. Thomas leapt up the stairs and into the bedroom. Jonathan was sprawled naked across blood-red satin sheets. Thomas smiled at him.

"You're so sexy," he said, offering the box of pie to Jonathan.

He took it and opened the lid, grinning. "Blackberry, my favorite. Thank you."

"Of course," Thomas said. He slipped out of his clothes and joined Jonathan in bed.

They kissed for a while, then Thomas held him as he watched the full moon from outside.

*Fuck. The full moon. A forced transformation. How did I not notice it?*

This wasn't good. He would soon shift under the gaze of the moon. If they were to move, it might delay the transformation—but by a couple minutes at most. And he didn't want to deny Jonathan, not during this moment of vulnerability.

*Shit.*

The clouds subsided, and the moonlight streamed in. He could feel the ripples starting—softly at first, but they would get more intense over the next few minutes.

"Tom..."

"I have to go."

"What? You just got here. Wait—" Jonathan grabbed his arm, then kissed his neck. "I want you inside me."

Thomas looked at him with surprise. *What did he just say?*

"What did you just say?" he blurted out.

"I said I want to bottom for you." Jonathan kissed him again and whispered, "Take me."

Thomas hesitated for a moment. *If I shift while I'm inside, I could hurt him. And he doesn't know about my shapeshifting abilities. What would he think?*

"I can't do this," he said with immense regret.

"Yes, you can. Look, I know I've said in the past that I'm strictly a top, but I want to be close to you. I need it right now."

After a moment of hesitation, Thomas said, "Let me close the curtains." He did so, and the room went dark. They began to kiss again. Jonathan's hands traveled across Thomas' abdomen, up his chest, to his neck, then his fingers tangled in Thomas' hair.

"Take me," Jonathan whispered.

The ripples were getting stronger now.

Thomas reached to the bedside table and grabbed the lube. He applied some to his cock and focused in on Jonathan. *Just focus on him, don't think about it just focus on him.*

Thomas kissed him passionately while he guided his dick inside Jonathan. The closeness brought a sense of comfort to Thomas. He wondered if it had the same effect on his lover.

Jonathan sucked in some air and exhaled a moan. Thomas kissed his neck as he went all the way in. Thomas breathed, circling his thoughts back to this moment. "Fuck, you feel so good," he gasped. The warmth around his cock was spine-tingling. The sensation of Jonathan's hard cock pressed against Thomas' stomach was enough to make him want to come right then. Gently, he pulled out.

"What?" Jonathan said. His voice was breathy and light.

"Nothing," Thomas said. He could feel the power of the moon turning him against his will. The ripples turned into pain as he suppressed them. *Just need a bit longer.*

Thomas thrust back in, deeper this time. He wanted to reach climax so that —

"Fuck," he shouted, then he let the ripples take over his body. The hair on his skin turned to thick fur, slowly but surely, all across his body. He grabbed Jonathan's neck and pulled him closer. "Look at me, just look at me, okay?"

"Okay," Jonathan whispered, then moaned as Thomas moved inside him.

Thomas could feel his dick growing bigger. He stopped thrusting and reached climax. He shot his cum deep into Jonathan's ass. Then he pulled out.

His dick was hot and sticky, and the smell of blood permeated the air. "Oh no," he whispered.

Then Jonathan noticed the blood. "Oh—" He reached for his ass and felt around, then lifted his fingers back to his face. It was too dark to see, but he could smell the blood. "Oh fuck. I don't feel so good..."

"Jonathan?"

When Thomas didn't get a response, he flicked on the light. Blood soaked the bedsheets, blending in with the satin. Jonathan's eyes were closed. *Fuck, he passed out.*

"Shit. Shit, shit-shit-shit," Thomas cursed as he paced about the room, growing still into the form he was trying so badly not to take on.

Thomas felt Jonathan's pulse—still there. "Oh, thank God."

He stumbled out of the bedroom and into the narrow hallway, his stature so tall that his fur grazed the ceiling. He entered the bathroom, not bothering to turn on the light. He grabbed some towels from the linen closet and hurried back into the bedroom.

And stopped in his tracks.

Jonathan was upright, an expression of sheer pain on his face. He arched his back in the most unnatural way, his spine cracking, and he screamed—loudly. Thomas could see his muscles expanding.

*No... It can't be...*

The screams in Jonathan's throat fell a few octaves, and now he sounded like an animal — like Thomas. The bones snapped and cracked under his skin, and his muscles grew larger as hair — no, *fur* — sprouted from his skin.

Thomas raced to Jonathan's side and tried to comfort him. Jonathan kept screaming in pain, and Thomas started to cry. He was panicking.

*Quick, think, think!*

Then he remembered the man he'd met in the woods. *I'll take him there. André will help me.*

He carefully scooped Jonathan into his furry arms and ran down the stairs and out through the front door. Thomas set Jonathan down in the backseat of his car. Jonathan's violent screams echoed throughout the neighborhood, and Thomas' heart pounded at the thought of being seen by neighbors in his half-formed lycanthrope state.

Thomas took the wheel and slid the seatbelt over his chest, clicked it in place, then slammed the door and raced straight toward the bridge over Lake Angular.

\* \* \* \*

Thomas managed to get a few miles into the woods before he had to stop the car. Jonathan was twisting and howling — he was *howling*. Thomas got out of the car then opened the rear door. The full moon disappeared behind a thick gray cloud, only to come back into sight a moment later. It shone its ethereal glow down upon Jonathan's sweat-soaked face.

Jonathan let out a preternatural howl. His jaw elongated into a muzzle, and his teeth grew and sharpened. As Jonathan transformed, so, too, did

Thomas. He let the moon take over and finish the process, releasing his hold and letting the ripples flow through him.

The seatbelt restraining Jonathan snapped and smacked Thomas in his right eye. With one final roar, Jonathan completed the transformation and burst the opposite door open. It broke from its hinges and went soaring into the forest. The door slammed into the base of a massive spruce tree and landed on the ground with a sharp, metallic crash.

Two sets of massive, bearlike claws gripped the sides of the car and a terrifying beast leapt onto the ground. The temperature dropped and snow began to fall as thick clouds shielded the moon once again. A piercing wind whipped through the night. He knelt beside the dented car, keeping himself out of Jonathan's line of sight—newly turned lycans were known to be aggressive.

The furry behemoth breathed deeply a few times, its breath crystallizing in the freezing air. It let out a few whimpers of lingering pain, then sniffed the frosted ground before pouncing into the trees and disappearing into the darkness beyond.

"Fuck," Thomas whispered. He closed his eyes as more hot tears formed. He gritted his teeth and kicked his tire. *"Fuck. Fuck! Fuck! Fuck!"* he cried, beating on his poor vehicle.

Then, without warning, his vulnerability ushered in the moon's influence and his wolf form took over his mind. He pursued Jonathan's wolf scent, following his footprints in the mud. A few minutes later, he reached the clearing he'd seen André in last night, and the tracks stopped. He sniffed the air, but the scent he'd had not a moment prior had vanished just as suddenly as the footprints. He had lost Jonathan.

Panicked, he set off for the castle on the shore.

# Chapter Three

Bramwell

The wind screamed in the bitter morning. Thomas had run until his legs had given in from the cold. He reached the cliff just in time. The drawbridge was lowering. He shifted back into his human form.

While Thomas sat on a large rock to rest, he admired the serene beauty of the castle, which had to be centuries old. Its looming pillars and towers stood high and erect, their rocky surfaces reflecting the full moon. The grand entrance, secured by the wooden drawbridge held by chains, gave sight to the lush courtyard beyond — and a particularly interesting-looking statue, though Thomas was too far away to make out the details. The castle itself stood on a cliff which was separated from Moore's Forest, and far below, craggy, sharp rocks and deep, freezing water spelled doom should anyone fall to their death.

Four men sauntered toward him from under the peaked archway and crossed the drawbridge. One of the men was André, who looked very pleased to see Thomas. One of the other men, a stocky bearded fellow with a bald head and a wide, sturdy frame, carried himself with the utmost confidence and power. He looked more like a leader when compared to André. The third man, to André's right, was much thinner in stature, his skin paler than fresh snow. His modest physique was slender and, though he had some muscle, it was very minimal. He had short white hair which was spiked straight up from his head. And the fourth man, to the bearded man's left, was the tallest of the group, with long black hair that danced in the wind and dark skin.

As seemed to be commonplace among this pack of lycans, all four men were nude. And while André's cock was the longest, the blond boy's was reasonably lengthy, albeit skinny, and the broad, bearded man's member was the thickest of the four, concealed behind a massive bush of dark brown pubic hair. Though it was freezing outside, somehow Thomas managed to get stiff. He tried to conceal it in embarrassment, unable to hide his acute arousal from the bearded man.

"Thomas!" André greeted him warmly, extending his arms and pulling him in for a hug. His cock slapped against Thomas' balls, but he didn't seem perturbed by the physical closeness. He let go and took a step back, then gestured to the three men behind him. "I'd like to introduce you to my chain-of-command—Rowtag Alonquin, the pack's guide, Krister Knopf, our watchman, and Gunter Talgden, our warrior. Rowtag is responsible for overseeing the pups, who you'll meet later, Krister keeps a weather eye on the forest and Gunter leads in battle. Comrades, this is Thomas Wright. I am hoping he will make a fine addition to our pack, should he choose to join."

The men nodded to Thomas, and Rowtag, the tall Native American, came near, grabbing his hand and clasping it with both of his. "Welcome, brother. I hope you will find companionship in our pack."

Then Krister, the slender boy with spiked hair, stepped forward. He glanced over Thomas' body with his dark gray eyes and said "Hullo" in an odd European accent. The last man, Gunter, pulled Thomas in for a great meaty hug. His thick member grazed Thomas', which was becoming hard once more. It was apparent that he was unequivocally attracted to this man. And for a moment, he felt embarrassment. But then, as Gunter's body closed the small gap between them and his hips made full contact with Thomas' hips, Thomas felt Gunter's cock throb against his own. Thomas was overcome with a wave of arousal. The man was so warm and comforting — *inviting*. He found himself reeling when Gunter released his grip.

"The rest of the pack are sleeping — getting their rest before the search party tomorrow," André said.

"Search party?" Thomas inquired.

"Yes, I'll tell you about that later. Come into our castle and let's talk for a while." He gestured toward the drawbridge.

"Wait, please," Thomas said. "I need your help My — my friend, he...I — I think I turned him. Into..."

"You turned him? Into a lycan?" Krister said with interest.

"I...I don't know." And Thomas didn't know, because he wasn't a lycan — he was a shapeshifter. And he didn't think shapeshifters could turn others.

"Gentlemen, Thomas here is gifted," André said. "He is a shapeshifter." The men gasped and looked at Thomas with fresh interest. "My boy, in my hundreds of years of studying kind like you, I have never come across evidence that shapeshifters can alter DNA in the way a lycan can."

Thomas felt a single tear drip down his cheek. "Then why is my friend wandering the forest as a werewolf?"

The men all looked at each other inquisitively.

"This cannot be," Gunter said, taking a step forward. "Shapeshifters do not possess the unique chromosome of a lycan. How could one turn someone else into a lycan when they were never one to begin with?"

André pursed his lips, thinking for a moment. "A lycanthrope has his own...what we call the Z chromosome, a part of his DNA which enables the transformation into another form—a wolf form. A shapeshifter, on the other hand, takes on a new form by touching it. So theoretically, a shapeshifter *could* take on the physicality of a lycanthrope by touching one in wolf form. But they are not compelled by any outside influence, such as the moon, to shift, because they lack the Z chromosome that a lycan possesses. The shapeshifter may be in the form of a lycan, but it is not a lycan."

"But I *am* compelled to shift under a full moon," Thomas replied.

"Into a lycan?" André asked.

"Yes, into a lycan. I am turned into one every full moon. But you're right, I am never compelled to transform into anything else on any given day."

"But how can this be, André?" Krister said.

"I don't know, but let's figure this out later and get on the lookout for this wolf. Use caution—the first turn is the worst, and he may not remember who he is."

\* \* \* \*

The party searched for over three hours with no result. Thomas felt immense guilt and panic. *What happened to Jonathan? Where is he now?* What *is he now?*

They came back to the castle. Thomas was fatigued and eager for rest. Ready to escape the frigid air, he was guided over the drawbridge and under the looming stone archway into a spectacular courtyard.

The statue he'd noticed earlier was breathtaking — a nude man bearing a spear in one hand and a shield in the other towered over the men as Thomas was guided around it. Its gaze seemed to follow him as they passed. He noticed the statue was also a fountain, and the water poured out of the statue's penis, giving the illusion that he was urinating. *An odd touch.*

The courtyard was divided into four squares, patches of grass and flowers and bushes nestled around marble benches. The greenery spread along the walls of the courtyard as well. On the opposite end, behind one of the benches, there stood an apple tree.

The men led Thomas through a smaller archway to the left of the grand entrance, through a hallway, and up a flight of stone steps. At the top was a narrower hallway lit with embers in silver plates suspended from the ceiling by chains. The orange light from the small fire flickered and lit the way just enough to see a couple feet ahead, then a sea of black until the next ember came into view.

At last, they reached a large wooden door at the end of the hallway. André turned the knob and entered, the others following behind him, Thomas in the rear. Thomas walked into a brightly lit study with bookshelves filled floor to ceiling and an elegant mahogany desk with several candles on the corners. Four chairs faced each other in a circle around a dark evergreen rug with a round coffee table in the center. A lit fireplace behind the chairs on the right side of the room flickered and warmed the space. Even the stone floor was warm in here.

"Please, have a seat," André said.

Thomas, Gunter, Krister and Rowtag took seats in the chairs, and André moved the chair behind his desk over to join the circle in front of the fireplace. He took a seat and clasped his hands together. The orange glow from the fire behind him eclipsed the edges of the chair, making him look more daunting than Thomas normally perceived.

"So, Thomas," André said. "To start off, tell us what brings you to Bramwell Castle this bitter fall morning?"

The wind howled outside the castle. There was a tall, narrow window behind the desk, with crimson curtains on either side, and on the outside Thomas could see snow falling at an angle. He was thankful he was no longer out there.

He cleared his throat and said, "I apologize if my demeanor is a bit off this morning. I've come to your castle because I'm lost. I have been for many, many years. I've lived alone for most of my life, and I've gotten close to no one. Except..." Then he shook his head. "Never mind. But something in me changed last night when I happened upon you, André. Something about the idea of not being alone in the universe, not being the only one plagued with this...well, you called it a 'gift', but I don't see it that way. Maybe more of a damnation. Anyhow, it changed my perception of my life, and how I've wasted so much time in this town. I want a purpose. I want to be a part of something. And that's why I'm here."

Thomas had to pause and collect his thoughts. He felt like crying but didn't want to project that kind of vulnerability in front of these strong, dominant men, especially not during the first time he was meeting them.

"We are happy to welcome you to our pack," André said, smiling at his company. "Your story is just beginning. I can assure you of that. Now, as for this friend of yours—do you know much about werewolves?"

"You mean other than Wikipedia and Hollywood movies? Not much," Thomas confessed. "Shit, I don't even know much about myself."

"A lycan turns a human into another lycan by way of intercourse—but only anal intercourse, and only with another male. Females cannot be turned. We still do not understand why, but the Z chromosome has no effect on their bodies. A lycan's semen has a silvery, reflective look to it, and it is in this semen that the Z chromosome exists. It latches onto the DNA of the human and, at the next full moon, transforms them for the first time."

Thomas swallowed and cleared his throat. "Yet somehow, I turned Jonathan into a..."

"Into a lycan," Krister said. "This is ridiculous, André! This man is not a shapeshifter—he is a lycan posing as one. Shapeshifters are nothing but myth."

"Once upon a time, you thought lycans were a myth, Krister," André said.

"Does this mean I turned Jonathan into a shapeshifter as well?" Thomas asked, fearing the answer. "Can my semen have that Z chromosome in wolf form?"

"I'm not quite sure, if I'm honest with you," André answered. "What little information I have on shapeshifting has not disclosed how a shapeshifter comes to be, or whether he can pass along his genetic abilities to another human mate."

"But at the very least, he must be a lycan," Thomas said. "I mean, that's what he turned into."

"What happened after you mated with this man?" Rowtag chimed in.

Thomas detailed the events that had occurred hours before, all while the four men around him stared wide-eyed, gasping at certain parts of his story.

When he finished, Gunter and Rowtag gawked at him then looked back at André, who said, "That's quite a story, Thomas. I have to admit, I'm not well-versed in the transformation rituals of shapeshifters. As I've said before, the knowledge of these beings such as yourself is very limited. You, Thomas, are an extremely rare creature, I hope you know that."

"What else can you turn into?" Rowtag asked. He seemed interested in what Thomas had to say, as did Gunter. Krister had his arms crossed and wouldn't make eye contact with him.

"Erm...well, lots of things. I've lost count of all the things I *have* turned into at one point or another. But the ones I shift into are a panther, a dove, and another human, as I demonstrated to André earlier last night. There's also a Bengal tiger, a crow, a viper and several celebrities I've met as well."

"You can shift into a snake?" Rowtag said, clearly mesmerized by Thomas and his abilities. "My ancestors had whispered of that kind of ability. The pack I come from believed in the existence of shapeshifters and sought to discover the way to develop that kind of power. My elders tried for centuries to shift into another animal, anything besides what they could already shift into—a wolf."

"How peculiar—and scary—that you can shift into another person," Krister mused. "If I had that power, I'd shift into anyone I saw on the street, just to confuse people."

"Believe me, I've indulged," Thomas said with a smile. "In fact, I have one other human appearance I like to shift into. His name is Evan."

André nodded. "When we met, Thomas had shifted into Evan to protect his true identity."

Krister scoffed. "You see? He's sly and untrustworthy. How can we let this stranger into our pack?"

"Krister, enough. This man is trustworthy, I can assure you," André said.

"How?" Krister said. "How can you know this...*shifter* is even real? If you can transform into a celebrity, then show me Claire Carter."

"I've never met her, but I can show you..."

Thomas felt the ripples rage through his body again, and this time he embraced them, releasing himself to the slight pain he'd grown accustomed to. An instant later, he was a different person.

Rowtag pointed at Krister and laughed. "Scarlett Rose! He's fucking *Scarlett Rose*! Oh my God! You look like a complete dumbass now, Krister!"

Krister gave him dagger eyes and turned away in a huff. On his way out, he said, "Don't come to me when he betrays you, André."

The room was silent for a moment. Then Gunter asked, "Who else can you be?"

Scarlett Rose smiled her trademark sly smile then her lips trembled, and she turned into Stephen Rovelo, then Ari Weaver, then back to Thomas.

"Wow, you've met all those people in real life? That's badass," Rowtag said.

"So, if it's all right with the rest of you, I'd like to get back to the original topic at hand," André said. "Thomas, do you know where Jonathan could have gone to?"

"No, I lost him in the woods and he...disappeared," he said, hanging his head. "He could have gone home, but like you said, a wolf doesn't remember who he is the first time. I know I didn't remember anything my first time, at age four."

"What did you first turn into?" Rowtag asked.

"I turned into a garden snake I had grabbed as it tried to bite me," Thomas said. "I got lost for days and almost got run over by a car. Eventually I returned to my human form on the neighbors' doorstep. It was the scariest moment of my life, and I remember all of it."

"Jesus," Rowtag said. "That's rough."

"Rowtag, I'd like you to assemble another search party and go looking for this man," André commanded, returning again to the main issue. "He's most likely afraid, confused and maybe a little angry. He'll be a danger to others, and we can't have a newborn wolf roaming around the area — the last thing we need is attention drawn to us. We might be able to spot him by his glowing eyes."

Rowtag and Gunter nodded.

Then André said, "I will go to the library in the east wing and find every book I can that discusses shapeshifters and bring them back here. We've got a lot to do, more so than before, and not much time to do it all, so I'll be reading up. Rowtag — go."

Rowtag stood, eager to fulfill André's orders. He left the study.

André stood from his chair and circled around the desk. Then he said, "Gunter, I would like you to accompany Thomas to our guest quarters. Be there for anything he needs and keep him safe. Thomas, you get your rest. We'll need you strong and ready when you wake."

Thomas and Gunter stood, walking toward the door. Thomas turned back. "André...thank you for this, for everything."

André drew close to him and rested a hand on his shoulder. "You're most welcome, Thomas. Now get your rest."

He kissed Thomas on the forehead and sent them off.

\* \* \* \*

Gunter led Thomas through the maze of hallways until they reached one with a series of doors on either side. He opened the first door on the left and ushered Thomas inside.

Thomas stepped into a dimly lit bedroom with a fireplace against the left wall and an enormous king-sized bed with a high-rise frame, surrounded by transparent white curtains. The room itself was a semicircle and against the far-right curve was a triangular stained-glass window. The flooring was hardwood and a massive rug covered most of it.

"Feel free to sleep where you like, on the bed or on the floor next to the fire," Gunter said. "I can stay in here with you if you'd like, or outside the door. Whichever is up to you. I'm fine with either."

Thomas was embarrassed to ask it, but he couldn't help himself. It'd drive him mad otherwise. "Um, well, I was wondering if you'd join me in bed."

"Oh?"

"Well, only if you want to. I'm very cold and your body is warm."

Gunter smiled and nodded. "Lycans tend to run a little hot to the touch. I couldn't tell if it was just the bitter cold or if your kind is not naturally as warm as my kind."

Thomas shrugged. "When I've slept with other men, they often commented on how warm I was. Maybe your temperature just runs hotter than my own."

"It's a mystery." Gunter grinned. "But that's what our books in the library are for — to learn everything about you that we can."

Thomas pulled back the heavy quilt and slipped under the sheets. Gunter gently shut the door then paced around the room to the other side of the bed, then lay down next to him. He pulled himself against Thomas' back and wrapped his arm around his chest.

"Good night, Thomas," he whispered.

Thomas closed his eyes, fearing what kind of dreams he might have. But Gunter's closeness gave him a sense of safety he hadn't felt in a long time. He drifted peacefully as the morning sun poured in from the window.

# Chapter Four

## The Monster

Rowtag sat perched on a tree branch in the heart of Moore's Forest. The pups were scattered around the perimeter below him. Alejandro, a bright young kid from Guatemala, was trailing a scent he'd discovered along a creek. He had joined the Bramwell pack two years ago, and he had an extremely talented nose. He could smell a fresh kill from miles away.

Max was to his left, flanking the outer edge of the cliff where the tides crashed against the rock. Max was loyal and ambitious, and Rowtag appreciated that. His sight caught even the subtlest of movements, the most indistinguishable of colors and the most faraway objects. He could see a boat on the sea before the average person would see it across the horizon. Though lycans could see better in the dark, their night vision was limited to about a thirty-foot radius. Max could see far beyond that, and he had also proved to be a great addition to the pack.

After Max was turned by his first love, a boy from his school, he was afraid of what he had become, and he'd worked hard to conceal his newfound power. Knowing his parents would not accept him, neither for being gay nor a lycan, he had fled his hometown of De Pere. He'd stumbled across Bramwell Castle and André had taken him in. He taught Max the ways of the Bramwell pack. Now sixteen, Max did his part in protecting the pack and was rewarded with a home and all the material things he could want for. It had been a welcome change.

The fourth among them was Rhyse, a formidable man with a quick wit about him. No one could best him, and he dominated everyone around him with an authoritarian disposition that other pack members found intimidating. Rhyse was especially remarkable. He could see through time. *"The constraints of space-time,"* he would argue, *"are the very thing keeping us from perfection. Would there be wars? Would there be famine, or death at all, if we could see forward through the hourglass?"* That's what he called it—the hourglass, a metaphor for the interwoven elements of time and space, and how earthly beings traveled through them.

Rhyse could see beyond one decision two seconds from now, or a week from now or a year. He could see all this and more...but he was never able to disclose this information, for he understood the drastic consequences that would transpire were he to alter the future before it happened. *"What could man destroy with such knowledge?"* he'd say. *"Evil is persistent and omnipresent. And if given the opportunity, evil will prevail."*

Nonetheless, he proved himself useful. What little information he could offer the pack of the future had saved countless lives over the years.

With a low grumble, Rhyse indicated to Rowtag that he had discovered something. Rhyse shifted into human form and they spoke under the full moon.

"I can see where he ends up," Rhyse said.

"Where is that?"

"He goes back to his house to retrieve something...valuable to him," he answered. "I can't say what it is, or when. But someone is following him."

"Alejandro..." Rowtag said. The young wolf whimpered in response. "Can you smell anything?" The wolf form of Alejandro shook its head. Rowtag turned to Max. "Maxi Pad!" Max's wolf scoffed at the joke. "Can you see anything?"

Another head shake.

"Damn...well, let's keep looking."

"We're a few miles away from the shore," Rhyse said. "I presume he either went toward the highway southward or back into town on the north end."

"Which do you find most likely?" Rowtag inquired.

"Neither," he said. "If I may offer...?" Rowtag nodded. Rhyse continued, "I believe he's still out here, somewhere in the woods, cowering under a tree."

"But according to your premonition—"

"How many times should I tell you, Rowtag, it's not a premonition, it's a foresight."

Rowtag rolled his eyes. "Sorry, so sorry. A *foresight*, then. According to your *foresight*, he backtracks to the north end of the highway, yes?"

Rhyse nodded.

"Right, then I think we should work our way back to the east side of the island and, once we check the opposite edge, wait near the highway until he comes."

Max shifted back to his human form. He was quite hairy, even in his natural state. In a deep, brooding voice, he said, "You mean we'll have to wait around all morning for this asshat to wander up the highway? What if he swims across the lake?"

"That's highly improbable," Rhyse said. "A newborn lycan swimming across an ice-cold body of water just to reach the other side which is connected by a manmade structure?"

"Enough of this!" Rowtag said in a deep, assertive voice. "You three go patrol the northern perimeter of the island. I will stay here and keep an eye out."

Max and Rhyse shifted again, and the three of them set out to fulfill Rowtag's order.

\* \* \* \*

Back at the castle, Gunter kept a sleeping Thomas in his warm arms. He stirred every now and then, and Gunter wondered if he was having a bad dream. He didn't want to wake the man, though, because he needed his rest, no matter the dream.

As they lay in the guest-room bed, Gunter's mind wandered. He could not help but admire this attractive young man's sculpted frame, his firm buttocks against his own cock... He wanted to love this man, and he couldn't figure out what was making his attraction so strong.

Perhaps it was a step of fate that Thomas had come to their pack, seeking help and companionship. Perhaps, it was a step of fate that he, Gunter, had stumbled upon this castle so many years ago, desperate for a safe place to rest his head. At the time, he had not thought much of his fate, or what the next eighty years with this pack would bring to his life, what good they would do. Lycans were not meant to wander alone —

their breed needed companionship, something to belong to and someone to share their life with.

Perhaps, he thought, this was why his attraction to Thomas was so irrevocably overwhelming. *Maybe this is the man I've been searching for my whole life.*

He shook the thought from his mind. *What a silly thing to consider. He can't be The One. Can he?*

But something about this man lying in his arms changed his mind. After many years of solitude, the moment Gunter had set eyes on this man, it was as if none of his previous history mattered. As soon as he had seen into Thomas' warm blue eyes, he was captivated, mesmerized, *transfixed.* And that was an unmistakable thing. This he understood, and he couldn't stifle it this time around.

Thomas turned in Gunter's arms, nuzzling his head against his chest. Thomas' cock grazed Gunter's, and this made Gunter rock-hard. Thomas' body was warm against his own. He embraced Thomas and pulled him closer, feeling his beating heart against his stomach and breathing the scent of his fine brown hair.

Though he told himself he wouldn't, he nestled his beard against Thomas' forehead and gave it a long, tender kiss. He rested his head on the pillow and breathed in tandem with Thomas. Their hearts synchronized and beat as one.

And for a long moment, Gunter at last felt love.

\* \* \* \*

Thomas awoke hours later, still entwined in Gunter's arms. He let out a yawn and stretched his limbs. He could lie there forever with Gunter keeping him company. The world could end and he wouldn't care. As long as he was here with this man.

But then reality hit him—he remembered what he'd done, and the moment was spoiled.

He sat up and covered his waist with the bedspread. He looked over at Gunter, who stared up at him with longing.

"You stayed," Thomas whispered.

"Of course I did," Gunter said gently. "You asked me to."

"Thank you. I'm embarrassed…"

"Why is that?"

Thomas blushed. "I had a dream about you."

Gunter smiled. "You did? Was it a good one?"

Thomas grinned. "Yes." He looked down Gunter's stomach and noticed a spot of silver in the hair below his naval. His cock was hard and a drip of precum traveled down his shaft. "Was that me?" Thomas asked.

Now Gunter was the one blushing. "No, not at all."

"Oh," Thomas sighed. He felt two things—relief and arousal.

"I can't help it," Gunter said timidly. "You're so…well, I don't mean to be frank…"

"I'm so what?"

"…beautiful."

Thomas smiled and looked away. Then he asked, "I know it's a castle and all, but is there a shower?"

Gunter chuckled. "Of course. André has done many updates throughout the castle. There's a bathroom through that door there." He pointed to the door near the fireplace.

"Very good. Thanks." Thomas got up and entered the bathroom.

\* \* \* \*

When Thomas emerged, hair damp and askew and the heat of the shower still clinging to his skin, Gunter was gone. His insides tumbled at the sight of an empty bedroom, but why should he feel so lonely? He'd spent the better part of his life alone — what difference should this one night make?

*Quite a difference indeed.* He slipped into the pair of jeans waiting for him on the edge of the bed. He felt at peace for the first time in ages, and that meant a lot.

He exited the bedroom and made his way down the corridor and into the adjacent passageway. The stone floor was like ice on his feet, and the hairs on the back of his neck stood up.

He emerged from the stairwell into the elegant ballroom he had seen earlier. He felt a tinge of worry as he stared at the vacant room. He wanted to talk to someone about the happenings from the previous night.

The midday sun leaked through the arched stained-glass windows along the opposite wall, streaming hues of pink, blue and green into the room. The wind howled outside, and judging by the chill he felt travel down his spine, he predicted it would be colder today than yesterday. October was chilly in Wisconsin.

Just then, a wide door on the other end of the room squeaked open and in came André. He was clothed now — a pair of gray sweatpants hugged his muscled waist. His furry chest was exposed through a loose white V-neck tee. His long brown hair draped over his shoulders. Thomas noticed, and found it quite amusing, that André's massive cock bowed out from in between his legs through the fabric of his pants.

"Ah, Thomas," he said and clasped his hands together. "So good to see you. Did you sleep well?"

"I did, yes," Thomas answered.

"Gunter told me you'd requested his presence through the morning. I'm glad he was able to ease your mind a bit."

Thomas' cheeks flushed. "Yes, I am, too. I wouldn't have gotten much sleep had I been alone. Have your men found anything regarding Jonathan?"

The door swung open a bit more and in came four men, only one of which Thomas recognized — Rowtag Alonquin, the tall Native American with sly eyes and a deep voice.

"Ah, just in time, men," André said. "Thomas and I were about to discuss the matter. Any news?"

They shook their heads. "Nothing, not even a scent," Rowtag said with chagrin. "We searched for six hours but found no sign of him or his wolf."

"I did, however, see something useful," one of the men said.

"Ah, yes. Thomas," André said, "this is Rhyse Griesbach. He is gifted in that he can see into the future as far as his eyes will let him."

"Really?" Thomas asked, hesitating to take André seriously. *Then again, why* wouldn't *a half-human, half-wolf be able to see into the future?*

Rhyse was just as unique in appearance. He had bright eyes that shimmered different shades of blue. Thomas inched closer to look deeper into his eyes. Rhyse stared him down with an inquisitive look. He looked as though he were concentrating very hard on something.

Rhyse had brown hair and thick brows which were furrowed in thought. His hair was pushed back, the ends of his curls hugging the sides of his neck. His jaw was square, and his thin lips were pursed. Perhaps most distracting was the man's chest, which stood out and gave him an authoritative quality.

"What did you see?" Thomas asked him.

"At some point today, Jonathan will go back to his home to retrieve something," Rhyse answered. "He'll stay there for about an hour, then he will leave."

"Where will he go after that?" Thomas pressed.

"I cannot say."

"Why not?"

Rhyse took a breath. "Because if you disturb the hourglass, the sands of time will not fall naturally."

Thomas looked at André, who elaborated. "He needs to decide how much of what he's seeing is information that can be disclosed to non-seers. In essence, if he were to alter time in a crude enough manner, eventually his eyes would deceive him."

Thomas nodded, then asked, "So can you tell me what time he goes there?"

"I cannot," Rhyse responded. "Such specifics would bend the hourglass too much."

"Uh-huh. I'm sorry, why is this helpful? If he can't give specifics on the future, what good does it do to have him see into it at all?"

Rhyse scoffed. "Silly boy...you could never understand."

"Try me."

Rhyse rolled his eyes.

"Look," André interjected, "before we get too heated, let's focus on the important information we have gathered from this. Thomas, I urge you to go back to Jonathan's home and wait for him there. Would you like some company?"

Thomas did want Gunter to come with him, but he had a feeling he should do this alone. "No," he responded.

Then there was a knock on the door and in came a group of young teens wearing street clothes — baggy pants, loose tees and sneakers.

"Thomas, these are the pups," André said.

"Hi, I'm Max," one of the boys said, stepping forward and extending a hand. Thomas shook it. "I lead the pups when Rowtag isn't around. Which isn't often enough." He laughed.

"Nice to meet you, Max," Thomas said.

"And this is Alejandro, he's a cutie — and my boyfriend." Max laughed again. "Then we've got Ricardo, Henry, Oscar and Sam," he said, gesturing to each of the boys.

"It's great to meet you all, and I'm sorry but I've got to get going…"

"Of course, get outta here," said Max.

Thomas bade his new acquaintances goodbye. André called after him as he exited through the door.

"Be safe, and come back soon," he said. "Oh, and Thomas! Don't rip those jeans apart. They're my favorite pair."

Thomas nodded and exited to the courtyard, passing by the erotic statue and walking under the archway, over the drawbridge and into the belly of Moore's Forest.

\* \* \* \*

It was windy and cloudy when Thomas emerged from the thick trees. It was Monday and he was supposed to be at work. *I'm not ever going back there, but*

*I'll deal with quitting later. More important things at hand...*

The highway was as busy as it always was in the mid-afternoon on a weekday. He caught a glimpse of something shiny out of the corner of his eye and, upon a closer look, was embarrassed to see his poor little car, its passenger door ripped off and lying in the ditch by the edge of the trees. It looked so sad... *Fuck me, what am I gonna do about this?* He had to take care of it—he couldn't just leave his car, this treasured piece of machinery that had made it through the last six years with him. And besides, he wouldn't mind keeping it, even though he was going to spend the foreseeable future living in a castle with a pack of gay werewolves.

*Jesus Christ...gay werewolves. A castle. A fucking castle! This is insane. Jesus Christ...*

Then, the thought of his little baby buggie, that tiny silver Hyundai Accent, sitting idle in the courtyard of Bramwell Castle made him snicker. *How absurd that will look!*

"Jesus fucking Christ," he muttered and chuckled to himself as he approached his car at the edge of the highway.

He ducked into the passenger seat and grabbed his phone from the cup holder in the center console. The screen was cracked on the top left corner of the display, but it seemed to work just fine.

He grabbed the clothes he'd balled up and tossed in the back seat, slipping into his shirt, socks and shoes, and tucked the jeans under his arm. He opened the phone app and called roadside assistance. *Thank God I went with that premium...*

He began walking toward the bridge north of the island while idle elevator music and the occasional *Did you know?* advertisement kept him waiting on hold.

A woman named Gina answered as he approached the bridge. The cars zooming by made it difficult for him to hear her. He explained that he needed a tow truck to grab his car and its passenger door from his location. Gina seemed perturbed and asked for more detail as to what had caused the 'accident.'

"Yeah, um..." *Fuck, what the hell am I gonna say?* "Uhh...I'm not sure what happened to the door, but I came back to my car from my buddy's house just now and for some reason it's off the hinge. No idea." He cringed, awaiting her response, but it was the best he could come up with on the spot.

"Was there anything stolen in the vehicle?" she asked in her long southern drawl.

"No, ma'am, nothing appeared to be stolen." He bit his lip.

After a few more questions, she said she'd have a truck sent out there within the hour. When he asked if he needed to be present, she said no. He thanked her. Then he hung up the phone as he reached the other side of the bridge.

The clouds parted and his body cast a shadow in front of him as the sun shone in the four o'clock sky. It was getting close to sunset, and Thomas wanted to hurry. For all he knew, Jonathan could have arrived and left his house by now.

About twenty minutes later, he reached the condo. Horrible flashbacks entered his mind as he was reminded of what he'd done the other night. *Oh Christ, Jonathan, I'm so sorry...*

He shook off the feelings of guilt and fear, and snuck around the condo, afraid of being seen by the neighbors. He found his way to the back-patio door, which, to his amazement, was unlocked. With a quick glance at the adjacent yards, he slipped into the house and closed the door behind him.

It was musty and dark inside. All the curtains were drawn, and there was a mess of clutter in the dining room — plates crusted with old food, glasses with a ring of hardened milk in the bottom. Piles of crumpled fast-food wrappers were strewn about the dining table and chairs. The kitchen was far worse.

The living room was the one part of the house that was kept neat. Jonathan liked to have sex on his couch, with the sixty-inch flatscreen mounted on the opposite wall. Thomas ascended the stairs to the second floor. He called out Jonathan's name, but there was no response.

*He's probably gone already...or he hasn't come yet.* It was frustrating to him that he didn't know which was true — or even if this Rhyse guy was telling the truth.

He reached the landing and noticed a trail of blood from the open bedroom to the dark bathroom on the other end. Chills ran down his spine as he recalled the gruesome details. How terrified Jonathan's face was...how fearful his shrieks were...

Thomas closed his eyes and slapped his head with his palm. "Stop it," he mumbled through pressed teeth. He heard Jonathan's screams echoing throughout the house now, as loud and clear as they had been the last time he'd stepped foot in this condo.

The sun was leaking in from the bedroom window, outlining the darkened, crusted trail of blood on the gray carpet. He knelt on the last stair, clutching his head with one hand and burrowing the other in the thick carpet beneath him. He groaned as Jonathan's screams grew more intense, the piercing cries of agony filling the house and shaking the walls.

Gradually, the screams faded. Thomas' head stopped pounding, his heart slowed down and he caught his breath. He wiped a tear from his cheek, inhaled and exhaled a few times, stood up with shaky legs and walked into the guest bedroom on the opposite side of the hallway, just to the left of the bathroom and far away from the bloodstained bed in Jonathan's room.

The guest bedroom wasn't much to admire — an empty metal desk and chair on the far wall, a closet on the other end by the bedroom door filled with tubs of junk and a navy-blue beanbag under the window were all that occupied the space. The blinds that covered the window were slanted and a few of the plastic ends were missing, letting streams of light in. The whole room was dusty and sullen.

Thomas sunk into the beanbag and pulled out his phone, scrolling mindlessly through his Twitter feed. After a few minutes of pure boredom, he tossed his phone on the floor and stared at the ceiling, letting his mind wander and his eyes fall shut.

\* \* \* \*

Thomas jolted awake around seven p.m. He reached for his phone and checked the time, yawning as he noted how dark it was outside — and how completely pitch black it was inside. But as he picked the phone up, he noticed just how far it was from him. He could have sworn he'd set it right by the beanbag.

When he unlocked the screen, he was taken to his text messages, not his Twitter feed.

A rush of chills ran through his body.

He turned on his flashlight mode and got up from the beanbag. He called out Jonathan's name in the darkness, but only heard his own groggy voice in return.

He thought about the pleasant dream he'd had involving Gunter and his stiff member grazed André's jeans. But the moment he stepped on dried blood, it deflated like a popped balloon.

He sulked down the stairs, arousal stifled by a grim realization. Halfway down, he stopped himself. *Was that rustling behind me?*

No, it was just his imagination running wild in the dark.

But then he heard it again—a faint stirring, as if someone were shimmying their feet across carpet.

His eyes widened, and he sucked in a breath, holding it in and straining his ears.

*There it is again!*

"Jonathan…" he whispered in the dark.

A low growl resounded in response, sending the hairs on Thomas' back straight up.

With a trembling hand, he turned his phone's light toward the banister and up through the railing.

The flashlight shone upon a pale, gray creature with crimson eyes and sharp front teeth. It had a long black cloak slung over its bony shoulders. It was emaciated, and its long, gangly arms arched downward from its hunched back. On the tips of its fingers were thick nails as yellow as a summer moon.

Its jaw dropped and a thin red tongue inched out as it hissed at him.

Thomas screamed and bolted down the stairs. He heard the creature thump over the banister and tumble down the stairs after him. He grabbed the front door handle, flicked the deadbolt lock, and yanked it open, racing down the porch steps and tripping on the grass. He fell to his knees and flipped, pushing his legs against the grass and crab-walking to the sidewalk. He saw the creature's blood-red eyes glaring at him from inside.

He ran through the streets of Jonathan's neighborhood and under the bridge, hyperventilating as he scrambled toward home in the dead of night.

# Chapter Five

## Full Moon

Thomas slammed the door shut and leaned his back against it, staring wide-eyed around his apartment. He had left it in a scramble—clothes were strewn about here and there and dirty dishes were piled in the sink.

But none of this mattered to him in his present state of mind. His heart was thudding inside his chest, his lungs sucking in air.

*What the hell was that thing? It wasn't human...and it couldn't have been Jonathan. Oh, God...did that thing get him?*

Paranoia swept his brain as he shuffled over to the kitchen drawer, pulling it out and withdrawing an old pack of cigarettes and some matches. No doubt they were stale, but he figured he wouldn't taste the difference.

He scrambled to the sliding balcony door and eased it open a crack, then struck a match against the box and lit the cigarette. He puffed in a gust of smoke. He closed his eyes as he exhaled, the evening wind on his cheek.

Thomas couldn't help but wonder where Jonathan could be by now. Had he made it home? If so, when? Had he gone there and left while Thomas was asleep? Was he still there when that monster arrived? Or was that monster there the whole time?

"Fuck," he cursed as he exhaled another puff of smoke.

He didn't know what to think. For all he knew, Jonathan could be dead. His lifelong curse, passed on through his own semen, had gotten the best of Jonathan and he was dead in a ditch somewhere, or drowning in Lake Angular, or —

*Or eaten alive by that creature.*

"You smoke?"

Thomas opened his eyes and felt a jolt of adrenaline. It took a second to register, but that voice was familiar.

It was Gunter, perched on the railing of his balcony, clearly admiring him with sensual eyes against the black backdrop and sparkling lights of the city.

"Yeah," Thomas said as he exhaled more smoke and flicked his ash down toward the street. "On occasion."

"Do you have another?" Gunter asked, stepping down from the railing.

Thomas nodded, then said, "Hold this." He gave Gunter his lit cigarette and ventured back to the kitchen to retrieve another. He came back and stepped outside in the chilly evening air, closed the patio door, and offered the cigarette and the pack of matches to Gunter.

Thomas noticed that he was dressed this time, and rather nicely, too — black slacks, a seafoam-green button-up shirt, and a black peacoat were draped over his body, which just this morning had been pressed against Thomas' own naked body.

"What are you doing here?" Thomas asked.

"I came to see you," Gunter replied.

"Were you following me?"

"No...Rhyse told me where you would be."

"Did you climb up here?"

Gunter smiled. "Yeah. This is your apartment?"

Thomas nodded. "It's not much, but it's home. Or, at least it *was* home."

"Do you mean you'll be moving into the castle with us?" Gunter seemed hopeful.

Thomas smiled. "Yeah, I think it does."

Gunter's eyes focused harder on Thomas, and he inched closer as he took a puff of his cigarette. "You look unsettled."

Thomas shrugged. "I..." He looked off into the distance, staring at a sign at an intersection below.

"You can tell me," Gunter said.

"I don't know what I saw. But..." He took a deep breath. "I saw something at Jonathan's place just now. Something...scary as hell."

"What was it?"

"I walked into an empty condo, and I was so fatigued from walking, I took a small nap in hopes that I'd wake up at the sound of him coming in. But it was dark when I awoke, and as I was leaving, I saw...*a monster.*"

"A monster?"

"I don't know how else to describe it," Thomas said, furrowing his brows. "It was tall and gangly — emaciated, it looked like — and it had...*fangs*, and a long, thin tongue like a snake's, and its skin was a murky gray color. The weirdest bit of it all was it had something draped over its shoulders — "

Gunter flicked his cigarette butt into the street below, grabbed Thomas by the waist and gestured to the sliding glass door. "We should discuss this in here."

"Why? Do you know what that thing might have been?" Thomas asked.

Gunter pulled him inside and closed the sliding door behind him. "I'm parched. May I have a glass of water?"

"Sure," Thomas said and retreated to the kitchen to fetch the water. "Take a seat wherever you'd like."

Gunter looked around the living room and noticed a huge flatscreen TV mounted on the wall near the sliding glass door. A big black sofa sat across from it. A large oak coffee table with a glass inlay sat snugly between the sofa, with two matching gray chairs on either side. The kitchen was separated by a half-wall a few feet from the back of the couch. He watched keenly as Thomas retrieved a glass from one of the cabinets and filled it with filtered water from the fridge. Gunter admired his physique from behind, and again his inner animal squirmed.

Gunter was sitting rigidly on the edge of the sofa. Thomas took a seat in the armchair nearest Gunter and gave him the glass of water. Gunter said thank you and took a swig.

"I think I know what you saw," he said tentatively. "I once encountered a creature like it so long ago—the night I was changed. And I have come in contact with them many times since. If I may, I'd like to tell you about them."

Thomas nodded, and Gunter continued. "First I'd like to tell you about my life, if I may."

"Of course," Thomas said.

"I was born in Milwaukee in 1903. My family emigrated to America in the late 1800s from Iceland. I would find out later in life, through years of genealogy and research, that I am a descendant of a royal family there. What I have yet to figure out, though, is why my family emigrated.

"My father and I never got along, perhaps because of his tendencies for physical altercations. He struck my mother on several counts, and once he even threw my younger brother across the room. His back landed against a brick fireplace and his neck snapped. He was paralyzed for the rest of his life."

"Jesus Christ." Thomas gasped.

"After that, my mother had had enough, and she made damn sure he was put behind bars. And he was, but not for long enough. My mother and I always got along well, until she discovered I was gay. I made the mistake of kissing a school crush goodbye in plain view. I didn't think anyone else was around. She turned away from me, and I never saw her again.

"We had lived a modest life, but I didn't have any money at the time. I went home, but she had the door locked and refused to answer when I tried to open it. I wanted so badly just to talk to her, even if she called me a string of hateful names—I just wanted to talk to her one last time. But she never answered the door. I started to cry and pound my fists, crying out for her. 'Please, *please answer!*' I begged — foolishly — and hammered my fists on that solid oak door until my knuckles bled.

"When sundown came, I figured I had to find somewhere else to go. My first try was at my then-boyfriend's house. But he lived with his parents still and just like with everyone else, I had to pretend he was a good friend of mine. And being seventeen years old in a time when homosexuals were scarcely discussed, we didn't establish any kind of relationship. All we knew was that we cared for each other, and we liked being intimate. My hope was not even to spend the night with him, but just to have someone to console me.

"But he refused to talk to me. He wouldn't let me in, even when he noticed my bleeding knuckles, and it was then that I discovered there was no such thing as love. I had decided it was a fallacy, a crude portrait of lies perpetuated by ones older than us. It was at that instant that I became a complete cynic.

"So I dropped out of school and began loitering around speakeasies. Rumor had it that some of them — and I hadn't figured out *which* ones — were where other homosexuals met to have sex. I wasn't even looking for that. I just wanted someone to talk to, someone like me. I managed to get into a speakeasy one night and the room I was ushered into was packed with older men, much older than myself at the time. One of them, Martin, grew fond of me, even after I offered myself to the group for spare change. Martin wanted to take me to his place. He was a widower and lived alone. He said I could stay with him as long as I needed. I agreed.

"But what he had in mind for me was so much more than just company. After some time, he tried to convince me to slip into BDSM apparatus and play along with him. When I said no, he screamed at me, *screamed* at the top of his lungs, that I was a no-good, nothing faggot, and that I belonged on the streets. It was then that I decided to part with him, but he would not let me. To this day, I can't remember how he got me unconscious, but I woke up hours later strapped to a bed in a room in the house I had no idea existed.

"He kept me as his sex slave for years. No one came looking for me—then again, I suppose no one would have, aside from my mother or brother or maybe my ex-lover. But it got increasingly worse. What started out as horrific, painful rape escalated into a frequent gang-bang. He brought in the other men from the speakeasy, and some men I had never met before. At that time, I had gotten so used to being violated that I didn't feel anything. My body and mind had gone numb, immune to reaction. I was stripped of individuality as well. So many times the men would get greedy and, after having their way with me, they'd force fellatio. I had more than enough chances to bite back, but I never did. I suppose I just did not care at that point.

"And then one day, I managed to unbind myself. I was malnourished and could not walk straight, but something within me was determined to break free, to live again. And I knew I had to do it alone, that I couldn't fight any of the men that would have been in my way one of those nights. I waited until dawn, just after Martin left for his day job, and I started squeezing my hand through the binds. They'd gotten looser as I lost more and more weight, and somehow Martin hadn't thought to tighten them. I dislocated my right thumb in the process, but within minutes I was free. I grabbed what things of mine that were still laying around—a few articles of clothing, which I put on right away, and a notebook with some sketches I'm surprised he never threw out. Then I made my way to his bedroom and retrieved an old shirt to throw on and all the money and valuables I could grab. I found a duffel bag under his bed which already had thousands of dollars in cash, and I filled the rest with spare change. Before I left, I helped myself to all the food in his icebox. I left all my dishes as they were, as a fuck-you I couldn't resist, and got out of there.

"I was free, free to breathe fresh air, free to roam the streets, free to eat whatever I wanted...free to *do* whatever I wanted. And what I wanted then was revenge. But I knew it would take some time, and I knew that in the meantime I needed to get as far away from Martin as I could, because he'd soon begin looking for me. So I used some change to buy a train ticket to its final destination, which was Chicago, an hour away. But it was a start, and Chicago was a big city. I figured I could at least stay there a week or so until I figured out my next move.

"So I booked a room in the nicest hotel, the Ritz, and I treated myself to the master suite. I had counted all the money in the bag while on the train and concluded — after three recounts — that I had sixteen thousand dollars with me, and that did not include the valuables. I remember thinking, 'Why on earth would anyone keep this amount of money in their home and not in a bank?' And then I realized that a bank meant a paper trail, which meant taxes and audits and so forth. I assumed that Martin was making money off me for those three years he kept me down in his basement, and what better way to spend it than to please myself for a change?

"I ended up staying there several months because I grew too comfortable. But then one day, I saw him in a crowd of people emerging from Union Station, no doubt looking for me. Why it took him that long to guess that I might have taken the train to Chicago was beyond me, but the instant I saw his face, I bolted. I stayed holed up in my room for the rest of the evening, and in the early morning, I gathered my things and checked out.

"After a few years of traveling from city to city, I wound up on the west coast in California. Oh, what a beautiful place! I was in love, and I planned on staying there for the rest of my life. But I needed something to do. I ended up working at a small bistro in a town not far from San Francisco. By day, I was a lonely, timid waiter who admired his male customers. By night, I was a bodybuilder-in-training, spending hours at a time exercising, working to get myself as strong as I could be. I wanted to know without a doubt that I could beat the life out of that monster and not be overpowered by him. And not just Martin, but anyone. I didn't want to give anyone the opportunity of physically dominating me.

"On my thirtieth birthday, I weighed in at two hundred and thirty pounds. My arms were bulging, my chest was three times as thick as it had been, and I was running the trails five miles a day. I was ready, and though I didn't want to leave California, I wanted to get my revenge. I told myself that I'd make it back home, next time maybe move into San Francisco or even to Sacramento or further north.

"With the six thousand dollars I had managed to cling onto, I made my way back to Milwaukee, hell-bent on revenge. But my long-awaited satisfaction would have to wait a moment longer.

"I emerged from the train station and found a lonesome boy sitting on a bench near the entrance doors. He seemed down on his luck and a little lost. He noticed me lighting a cigarette and asked if he could bum one of mine. I nodded and produced another from a pack in my bag. He went out of his way to thank me multiple times, reiterating that it meant the world to him and that he needed one. He seemed so desperate to make it apparent to me that he was thankful. I found it peculiar and humbling, though I couldn't help but feel for the kid on some level.

"After I finished my smoke and had a brief, albeit uncomfortable conversation with the boy, we parted ways. I watched him travel down the moonlit road into the dark of the grim, hollow city. I walked the other way, northbound.

"As I approached the bus stop on the other end of the street, I heard a short, loud scream echo from an alley on the opposite side. The street was dead, lit by sporadically scattered deep-orange lights. The alley in question was snug between two derelict apartment blocks.

"I can't say I was in the right frame of mind, but something within me felt the need to help this person on my own. I made my way across the street, all the while staring into the black abyss between those two towering buildings. As I grew closer, the sounds that filled the air resonated within me, and primal instinct kicked in as I realized what was happening.

"The sounds of meat grinding against bone, the slurping of blood, and, as I came closer still, the smell of fresh blood intermingled with the urine and feces in the alley swirled around me. I became overwhelmed and my heart thudded, my palms sweated. I got close enough to see the fresh-spilled blood of the monster's victim shining against what little light could leak in from the street.

"The monster was bald and bony, and had milky-white skin and fangs that jutted out from its chapped lips, which were slathered in blood. It was naked, a humanoid being covered by a thin silk cloak black as night. My eyes traveled from the monster looking up at me to the victim in its grasp. To my horror, it was Martin, the one who had driven me to become what I was in that very moment.

"I felt overwhelmed with anger. Anger at this creature that had beaten me to this bastard's punch. Angry that I was deprived the satisfaction of murdering the one foul human being that had altered my life so drastically. *Furious* that all I had worked toward had been squandered by this thing in front of me.

"I reached into my pocket and produced a small retractable knife. I flicked it open and, with a ferocious battle cry, I charged at the monster with rage in my heart and adrenaline in my veins. I forced the blade into the monster's belly and felt it squirm as it recoiled under my weight. I pinned it to the ground and withdrew the knife, then stabbed it again, and again, and again, until it could shriek at me no more. For good measure, I slit its throat and watched it writhe in pain as its last breath escaped from its dry lips.

"I gathered myself and sucked in a few harsh breaths, wiped the perspiration off my brow and loomed over Martin's lifeless body. I felt defeat knowing that he would never see my face, never see what I had accomplished in spite of him. And I felt humiliated that I had let this man get to me like that, to fear for my life and forever strive to become so strong, so powerful, so driven...all for this one man who had not given me anything, but rather had taken everything away from me. I felt ashamed and embarrassed, and I knew in that moment that I was a complete fool.

"So I knelt down in fury and stabbed his corpse until I could not exert any more energy. The sound of his insides wriggling about my blade was the most satisfaction I could have gotten out of that situation, and to this day I feel that it was justified.

"When I was done, I threw myself back against the brick of the building and cried. I was drenched in blood and sweat. I cried for what felt like hours, and when I had collected myself, I opened my suitcase, changed my clothes and left the alley. I got on the next bus. I didn't take a second glance at where its destination was, because I didn't care. I just needed somewhere to go.

"Curiously enough, the boy I had given a cigarette an hour ago was sitting behind me. He tapped my shoulder and sparked up a conversation. It was just the two of us on the bus, and we rode it until it stopped at Oshkosh. He took me back to his shoddy apartment, where I confessed what I had done. I started with my story, as I've been discussing with you now, so as to provide context. I could tell he felt for me, and when he opened up his secrets after I was finished, I felt for him. We drew close to each other, and we made love.

"That was the night I was turned."

* * * *

Back at the castle, André sat in his study with Rhyse, his hands clasped together in thought. Rhyse was focusing on something distant, his eyes closed and brows furrowed together. André cleared his throat in an effort to pull Rhyse back to the present.

"Can you see anything substantial?" André asked.

Rhyse nodded. "I can see them. They're getting closer. One of them nearly attacked Thomas."

"Is he all right?"

Again, Rhyse nodded. "He is with Gunter back at his apartment. They are discussing personal stories... The weak one has fled Jonathan's home. He is on his way here, as are the rest of them."

"What do they want?"

"They're searching for..." He became frustrated, and closed his eyes once more to see forward again.

"Searching for what? Solace? Are they in trouble? Or perhaps searching for us specifically? Are we in danger?"

"Not imminent danger, no," Rhyse responded "They are searching for help."

"Help? With what?"

"I cannot see. I guess we'll have to wait and find out."

\* \* \* \*

Thomas got up and retreated to the kitchen, emptying his glass in the sink and searching his cabinet for the right liquor. "You want a drink?" he asked Gunter.

"Please," Gunter answered. "Nothing too strong. I can't control my shifts if I drink too much."

Thomas threw together a cocktail — gin and tonic for himself and spiced rum with cola for his guest. He went back into the living room and sank into the couch, offering Gunter his drink.

"Did you speak to him afterward? The boy?" Thomas asked.

Gunter shook his head. "He left in a hurry, said he had to leave but didn't give me an excuse. He slipped out of his apartment through the bedroom window, scaled the side of the building and fell down into a shrub. He scurried off toward the downtown area. He had told me I could stay as long as I wanted.

"But the moon was full that night, and as I gazed out his open window, following him with my eyes, the moon's brilliant gaze sent ripples through my body. I shifted then. It was painful—the most painful experience I'd ever had—and it was slow, gruesome. I could feel my skin rip as it expanded, my muscles tear as they did, too, and I heard the sounds of my bones breaking as they elongated. I felt I might pass out from the pain, but almost as instantly as it had happened, it was over.

"I stood there in his bedroom, staring at myself in his floor-length mirror, appalled at what stared back at me. I was stricken with disbelief. I was a monster, a furry, humanoid creature with a muzzle and sharp teeth and claws. I noticed as the pain subsided that it was replaced with a wave of immeasurable pleasure. It was so overwhelming that I noticed a string of silver trickling from my hard shaft into my matted fur. Curious, I dug a claw into my pelvic fur and grabbed a string of the matter, examining it closer. It was semen, but its consistency had changed."

Thomas took a breath as arousal swept his body. He felt himself throbbing against the inside of his jeans. He wanted so badly for this beautiful, scarred man to be inside him. But it wasn't the appropriate time. He shifted his position, moving his cock to a more comfortable angle.

Gunter went on. "That creature you saw, like the one I encountered so many years ago, is a Nightstalker. They hunt humans at night when the sun cannot hurt them to drink their blood and stay alive. Or as alive as they can be."

"They're immortal, too," Thomas said.

"Yes," Gunter responded. "And not much will kill them. Vampires are immortal short of the sun, a stake in the heart, or a beheading—they will not die. Not even starvation will kill them. They just go into a hibernation state until another vampire resurrects them with blood. It's a ritual that requires the life of a living person. It's disgusting. But Nightstalkers—all they exist to do is kill, and a stake in the heart doesn't faze them. The sun is still damaging but less potent. Really, with Nightstalkers, the only way to kill one is a beheading. They are a threat to not just humans but us as well, because they want to eradicate us. But there is one other thing that can kill them—a lycan's fangs are poisonous to a Nightstalker. They die within minutes of being bitten."

"So Nightstalkers are vampires then..." Thomas mused.

"They are vampires that have succumbed to their evil nature. Ordinary civilized vampires don't look like that—it's probably why you were so startled. You must never have seen one before."

"No, I haven't. I've met a couple vampires—one was before they were known to the world—but they looked like people, just paler."

"Exactly—a vampire that drinks synthetic or animal blood retains their human beauty," Gunter said. "But Nightstalkers, the vampires that drink human blood, become deformed as they age. They also become far more powerful and near-invincible."

"So if not much can kill a Nightstalker, does that mean you didn't kill the one in the alley?"

"I don't know. I don't want to know."

"What is the pack doing to stop them?" Thomas asked.

Gunter grinned. "Don't worry, we've got our best men following their every footstep. Rhyse has a unique gift, and it helps us track them. Though he is inhibited by the master Nightstalker, Andromeda, and her powers. She can project false visions into his mind and mislead him. That is why our runners, Rowtag and his pups, track them around the city at night. We're on the cusp of learning what they've come to Creston Bay for."

"Where did they come from?" Thomas asked.

"This particular coven has migrated here from Russia, a remote village in the heart of a never-ending snowstorm."

"Are there more of them?"

"Rhyse cannot see. Andromeda is hiding something."

\* \* \* \*

After another round of drinks and some more sexual tension, the conversation shifted back to Jonathan.

"You probably know the process of a transformation by now, no?"

Thomas shook his head, then rescinded his answer. "Well, maybe...it has something to do with my semen..."

Gunter smiled. "I must admit, I'm surprised this is the first time you've changed someone."

Thomas flushed. "Well, er... I have been the giver, but never as myself."

"How do you mean?"

"I have this...persona. Evan Winston." Gunter nodded. Thomas continued, "I shift into him when I'm in the mood to top. I feel more confident that way."

Thomas noticed Gunter's expression change into disapproval.

"You don't need to feel that way," Gunter said. "You're sexy and..." He inhaled. "...inviting."

"I could say the same about you," Thomas replied with a smile.

"Earlier you said, *'whenever I'm in the mood to top.'* What does 'top' mean?"

Thomas looked up and smiled. "Finally, something I know that you don't!" Gunter laughed. "A top is the one who is inside the man, the bottom is the one that receives the man's cock."

"Oh. I have not heard that before."

Thomas continued. "Anyway, I tried being on top when I first became active, but I found that I couldn't stay hard. Instead I put on my Evan Winston costume and suddenly, I had all the confidence I could ask for, and I was able to perform. I came inside the boy I lost my virginity to—as Evan."

"Hmm. Interesting," Gunter said. "And your semen, if you don't mind my asking, is it silver in human form as well as in lycan form?"

"No, just in lycan form," Thomas said. "Otherwise, it's...well, normal semen."

"So one could surmise that you turned him because your semen changed consistency as you were shifting. You could turn someone with a lycan's semen, but not your own in human form."

"Holy shit," Thomas said. "That makes so much sense."

"I do wonder, how did you turn into a lycan?"

Thomas cleared his throat. "Well, my first time was with a lycan. I didn't know it at the time, but I think by touching him, I...absorbed some of his power and took it on as my own. Because he never topped me, I topped him as Evan. But of course I did touch him, so..."

"Right..." Gunter mused, stroking his beard. Then he smiled. "What was it like? Is that too forward of me?"

Thomas grinned back. "Not at all. It was...*hot*. We made out for a while, then moved onto blow jobs, and he let me top him even though he'd mentioned he had never taken someone as big."

"Oh?"

Thomas laughed. "Yeah, Evan's hung. Anyway, we had sex for a long time — the boy was a champ. Eventually I decided I wanted to come, so we got ourselves off."

"By that you mean...?"

"You have never heard of that before? I thought that was a saying that had stood the test of time."

"If it is," Gunter said, "I've managed to skim through life without hearing it once."

"Well, 'get off' means to come...or ejaculate."

Gunter laughed. "I do know what 'come' means."

"Good, because I'd be worried in that case," Thomas said with a chuckle. "So we got ourselves off instead. And I'm glad we did because watching him work himself and then shoot his load was the hottest thing I've seen to date. I still have the image in my head, and sometimes I jerk off to the thought of it."

"How many men have you been with?" Gunter asked. "I'm sorry if it's too invasive. You don't have to answer if you don't wish to."

"No, it's fine, I don't mind. At this point, I think about seven hundred or so. I don't know if you've noticed this, but the nice thing about the ability to shift is when your — forgive my crudeness — when your hole widens from a thick cock and you shift into a lycan, or in my case, whatever I would shift into, upon shifting back, your hole tightens to its normal size. Which is excellent for working the street corner. Sleazeballs pay big money for virgins. They don't have to know you're not actually a virgin, just that you feel like one."

Gunter swallowed the last of his drink and cleared his throat. Then he said, "I must confess something to you, dear Thomas..."

"Fire away," Thomas said.

"I desire you. I am mesmerized by your beauty, and I've been fixated on your presence since the first night you'd arrived at the castle. And when I held you as you slept that evening... I could not stand it. I had to tend to myself the moment you stepped in the shower. And I must admit, considering all I've gone through in my life, and what I've just told you... I thought I no longer believed in the possibility of love. But something about you is changing my mind.

"I do still have my reservations. For example, I don't know that I am ready to commit myself to a future life with a man, no matter how intoxicating he may be to me, how wildly he drives my senses and makes my cock pulse with sexual desire."

A wave of arousal rushed through Thomas' body. He looked down at the empty drink in his hand and swirled the melting cubes around with his straw. Then, after a long pondering moment, he took a breath and responded, "I should say thank you. No one has ever shown an interest in me like you have, and I can admit that I feel the same toward you."

Gunter smiled. After a brief pause, he said, "Can I ask you one more question?"

"Shoot."

"Do you like being a shapeshifter?"

Thomas was caught off guard by this. He thought for a moment, then answered, "There are perks to it and advantages, but I've been on the run my whole life. Because I don't age, I'll always look the same unless I shift into someone else. And by that time, I've started a new life for myself. I've been running and running forever, and I don't want to spend the rest of eternity doing the same. And I don't want the same for Jonathan. If I did turn him, what I gave him was a curse. The curse of immortality."

"Is that really what you feel?" Gunter's eyes were soft.

Thomas looked down again at his glass. "I need another," he said, and got up for a refill.

While he mixed his drink, he thought about what he'd just said. Did he believe immortality was a curse? *Just look at your life. Look at what it's done to you.* He went back into the living room, his mind a racing swirl of emotions.

"Gunter..." He scooted toward the edge of the couch and looked his guest in his stunning brown eyes. "What I said is true. I feel that immortality is a curse because of what my life has been. But maybe someone can change my mind. Someone like...you."

"You mean that?" Gunter said.

"I gravitate toward you. You entice me, and I, too, can't get you out of my head. I want to love you, and I want to be yours. But I need time — just a little, but I do need some time to adjust to this new life I'm walking into. I need to settle my issue with Jonathan first, and I need to grow comfortable. Part of me thinks being with you would just make it harder, but another part of me wonders if it could be a great help instead."

Gunter smiled. "That's quite flattering. I think it's best to wait and see, rather than take the risk."

Thomas nodded. He furrowed his brows and, with his arousal taking over, said, "We don't have to have sex, but could you hold me while I sleep again?"

Gunter smiled. "Of course. I was hoping you would ask."

They shuffled into the bedroom, and Thomas began to strip down to his underwear. Gunter did the same and joined him in bed.

"Goodnight, Thomas," Gunter whispered.

"Goodnight," he replied.

After a moment's hesitation, Gunter gently grabbed Thomas and pulled him closer.

# Chapter Six

## Closer

Thomas woke early in the grasp of his companion. He stroked Gunter's arm, thinking about a future with this man.

*What will it look like? Maybe a lifetime with the pack will bring me happiness. Then again, maybe it won't. But this man...this man can bring me happiness.*

He struggled with these thoughts as he slid out of bed, quietly, so as not to wake Gunter. *If you give yourself the authority to do this, leave your life behind and start anew, you also need to give yourself permission to open yourself up. Let someone in for a goddamned change.*

He pondered this and began to make breakfast — eggs and bacon. *And maybe some toast, too. Fuck, I don't know what I want to do.*

He decided it'd be best to spend the day alone, away from the thrill and excitement — and anxiety — about a new opportunity. *And what an opportunity it is! To spend my days with others similar to me, to belong to something bigger than myself, and to give a chance to this incredible man...*

Then Thomas looked around the kitchen and into the living room. This small box was all he had to call home, but it was a nice home. A comfortable home. A familiar home. *Am I willing to give this up? I'm content here. I like it here. This pathetic one-bedroom apartment is all I've known for the past fifteen years.*

Just then, anxiety set in — the anxiety of leaving something. The fear of jumping off that cliff and into the dark unknown.

*But you've done this many times before – and Gunter will help you.*

And he would, Thomas knew it. Gunter was kind, and caring, and compassionate. And deeply, deeply scarred.

*Can I heal him? Can he heal* me?

He scrambled the eggs and mulled some more, wishing that Gunter would wake up and come into the kitchen. This craving opened Thomas' eyes a bit, and his vision of the future became a little clearer.

But he still had things to consider and do.

He ate his breakfast in solitude, all the while fantasizing about the man in his bedroom. He wanted him. That craving also opened Thomas' eyes.

He made up a plate of eggs and bacon for his guest and wrapped the plate in tin foil. Then he wrote 'Gunter' on a sticky note, stuck it to the foil and set the plate on the dinner table. After a quick shower, he dressed and exited the apartment, giving the bedroom door one last glance on his way out.

The first order of business was to quit one of his jobs. He figured he'd keep one of them, to have spending money. He wasn't sure how André handled income, or if he happened to have a vast fortune he was sitting on, but Thomas wanted to keep a little bit of individuality in this process.

He made up his mind about moving in with the pack just then. He yearned for a sense of belonging, and he was lonely. *What can it hurt? If you don't like it, you can always leave. You have agency, Thomas.*

And he did. That was why he was doing this — it was of his own accord. He knew this deep down, and he thought about it while he left the apartment building and headed toward the coffee shop — his second job.

He ordered a vanilla latte from the barista, his coworker and friend Shalese. She said hi enthusiastically and made casual conversation with Thomas while she made him his latte.

"Don't you work tonight?" she asked.

"Yeah, I do," he replied. "Can I tell you something? Something that needs to stay between us."

"Of course, darling," she said, handing him the latte she had just finished. She tapped in one of her coworkers to man the front counter and stepped into the empty break room with Thomas.

"All right, go," Shalese said.

"Okay, so, get ready for this," Thomas said.

She closed her eyes. "I'm ready."

Thomas grinned. "I'm quitting my call center job and moving in with the lycans."

Her eyes opened and widened. "What? Thomas!"

"What?"

"That's fucking awesome! I'd love to meet them. Though I've heard they despise humans — not sure if that's true or fake news."

"They don't, actually," he replied. "This pack is very kind to me, and they don't hate humans at all, because they are still human themselves."

"I'm just curious, with you being immortal and all, how long have you been alive?"

"Sixty-two years."

She gasped. "Wow...and you look the same. How did you get turned? Is that rude of me to ask?"

"Um...it's a long story." He sipped his coffee and watched her reaction.

"Hmm..." She folded her arms and leaned back. "I didn't realize there were other lycans in the area — that's so cool!"

"You aren't afraid of them being dangerous? Because they can be...though not as dangerous as vampires."

"Nightstalkers..." she mused. "I've never met one in real life, but the movies scare the shit out of me. I do wonder what it would be like to encounter one, though."

"They'd suck your blood and leave you to die," he said. "Lycans are much more nurturing, I've found. The pack leader, André, has been nothing but kind to me. He's fascinated by me for some reason." Again, Thomas felt bad for telling a half-truth, but he wasn't ready to reveal himself. If shapeshifters were so rare, if word got out, who knew who'd come looking for him? What kind of danger would he get himself in? *No, playing it safe is the better way to go.*

"Hmm...lots to think about," Shalese said.

"Please don't tell anyone about all this. And whose business is it, anyway? You know?"

"I promise I won't. But real talk, Thomas, don't tell anyone else," she said, setting her palms on the table. "Don't. Just...keep a low profile. You don't want the crazies coming after you."

"By crazies, you mean...?"

"Religious zealots who believe lycans are of the devil! Paranoid gun owners who can't wait to fire at something in the name of personal freedom. Not to mention the sport of it all—lycan hunting. It's a thing, and it's scary. They murder lycans and take pictures of the body, and then they post it online for the whole world to see. And you think Facebook gives a shit about lycans' rights? About what's basically genocide? These things are *real people,* and even though we know about the existence of lycans, the world is so corrupt and fucked up that humanity can't see that lycans are people, too. It's disgusting. Okay, rant over."

"No, I enjoyed it," Thomas said with a smile, and took another sip of coffee. "Tell me how you feel about vampires."

"Don't even *get me started* on those things," she said. "Vampire rights are just as important as lycans' rights."

"Didn't realize you were our queen," he said with a laugh.

"Of course! I hate the way other people are treated. Lycans and vampires are a minority just as gay people are." Thomas didn't know how he felt about that, but he stayed quiet. "They deserve their own rights."

"Even though vampires are murderers?"

"Not all vampires are evil," she said, pointing at him. "Not all of them kill people. Some of them are good and drink animal blood. I read a few articles. Not ones found on Facebook, *real* articles in news apps. They talked about just how bad the hate crimes are against lycans. Vampires, too—good people who got turned against their will or perhaps willingly got turned, but don't drink people's blood, they drink synthetic blood or whatever—my point is, there is good and evil in the world, and evil persists across both spectrums. The vampires who kill and get away with it because 'it's in their nature' — gimme a fucking break. I swear to God — "

Thomas laughed. He loved his best friend's tangents.

"I'm getting off topic. Anyway, what I'm trying to say is that you don't have anything to be afraid of as far as 'coming out' goes — remember what it was like for you coming out as gay?"

"Yeah," he said. "I do. It was...difficult, to say the least. I came out to everyone in the eighties."

"Ouch," she said. "That's rough."

"Yeah. The world hated gays back then. Our own president watched as people died from AIDS and did nothing but preach abstinence. People got murdered — brutally, I should add — and pop culture mocked gays as off-brand. It was a cruel world. People think about the eighties as if it was the height of civilization, but it just wasn't that way for me. Sure, music was at its peak and movies were getting better, but it wasn't until gay marriage was legalized that I saw true change in the way people thought about gays."

"The same thing happened with supernaturals when they 'came out of the closet,' so to speak. Not to degrade your coming out as gay, gosh no, I didn't mean that — "

"I didn't think you did," Thomas reassured her.

"Okay, good. But yeah, same thing happened with the vampires and the lycans once they were discovered and documented."

"We'd stayed private and secretive for centuries, with nothing but myths surrounding our existence, and now the whole world knows about us. And it's all thanks to the fucking Internet."

"Yeah," she said with a sigh.

"Oh!" he exclaimed. "I have other news…"

"Do tell, darling!"

"There's a man…"

Shalese gasped. "No way. Who?"

Thomas shook his head. "You don't know him. He's wonderful, Shalese. He's big and burly and hairy, and I just adore him. He's kind and complex, and I think he likes me, too."

"That's great! I'm so happy for you!" She squealed.

He smiled. "Thanks. I'm still not sure that I want to trust someone like that—"

"What do you mean? This guy is hardcore into you, as you said, and you wanna just let that big fuzzy bear of a man walk out on you? Don't be silly."

"I just don't know that I'm ready to have another relationship."

"Why not?" she pressed.

Thomas couldn't answer her question. He thought for a minute and came up empty-handed. "I don't know."

"Well, figure that shit out, because he sounds great to me. And it would be good for you! You've been playing around with Jonathan for years now. It's time to get serious."

*Right. Jonathan.*

Thomas decided then that he would be on his way. He'd done what he came here for, which was to get clarity on the situation.

"All right," he said, getting up. "I should get going. Thank you for this, it was a big help."

"Of course, darling, any time." Shalese gave him a hug, and they left the break room.

Thomas made himself another latte to go then dipped out of the shop. He pulled his phone out and dialed the number for his supervisor at the call center.

She picked up immediately. "This is Shannon."

"Hi, Shannon, it's Thomas. Listen..." He took a breath.

"What?" she said.

"I need to quit. My life has changed in the last few days and I—"

"Are you *fucking* kidding me, Thomas? You're ditching out on us again when we're short-staffed and busier than ever? How dare you?! Don't show up at work, then call me the next day saying you're done. You're despicable."

Thomas took another deep breath and closed his eyes. He was stopped at the corner of Walle Avenue and College Lane. The traffic around him was overwhelming, and he wished he was back at his apartment for this conversation.

"Look," he said, deciding at the last minute to say *fuck-it-all*. "I'm a lycan and I'm moving in with a pack of other lycans like me so I can't fucking work there anymore. Sorry. Also, you're a massive bitch." Then he hung up.

He was very satisfied with himself in that moment. He felt free.

* * * *

Around eleven o'clock, Thomas got a call from the repair shop his car had been sent to. The man on the other end told him that his car was not worth fixing.

"The door alone is over a thousand dollars for a brand-new one, or you could take your chances at a junkyard," the man explained. "But this model is very old and finding parts is gonna be tricky. You're better off just taking the insurance money and getting a used car."

Thomas was let down by this because the little Hyundai had been in his life for six years now. He had an attachment to it. But he supposed a new chapter in his life could start off with a new car. *Why not, right?*

He figured he would wait to hear from the insurance company before he looked for another car. He put it to the back of his mind and thanked the man on the phone, then hung up.

He looked around, seeing the city with fresh eyes. He watched as the pedestrians walked by, the cyclists zipped down the street, the impatient cars honked at each other. Downtown Creston Bay was lively and exciting. Thomas loved walking the Avenue, so that was what he did for the rest of the day.

He wandered into his favorite shop, Clint's Books, and had a look around the Religion and Philosophy section. He perused a few books about the origins of certain religions, and one about Freud. He carried the Freud book around with him while he checked out the romance section. Nora Roberts, Danielle Steele…he picked up *The Witness* by Roberts and read the inside jacket summary. Deciding he liked it enough, he found his way up to the front counter and paid for his new books.

Thomas sat down for a while and read Nora Roberts. He liked her writing style—it was quick and precise, and detailed, too. He read for a bit and let his mind wander. *What do I want to do? Do I give a chance to Gunter and take his hand in all this? What would that mean for my future?*

All this doubt was driving him crazy. He knew he just had to make up his mind already, decide on a course of action. He watched pedestrians walk by outside. Expensive cars rushed past, honking at a group of young adults crossing at a red light. He noticed the sun was at its peak — it was past noon.

He got wrapped up in his new novel, and before he knew it, it was three p.m. He figured he'd better get going — stretch his legs a bit.

He wandered into the record store across the street, perusing the alternative section. Metric, Coldplay, Lights, the new Imagine Dragons album. While passing the Pop section, he spotted a vinyl from an artist he'd never heard of — James Tyler. The album on display was *Timeless*, which had a peculiar and intriguing cover. A man, presumably James Tyler, stared at Thomas with striking brown eyes. His head was dissolving into a noisy fire-truck-red background. The edges of his face sparkled with what appeared to be glitter on the artwork. *Shit*, he thought. *I should snag that*. Thomas was always up for hearing a new artist.

So he did, and took it up to the register. He paid, handing his cash to the cute clerk with curly brown hair and big black-rimmed glasses — a total hipster.

He headed home with his new belongings under his arm, hoping that Gunter was still there in his bed. He realized just then how much he'd missed the man — and the rest of the pack. Rowtag was adorable and had leadership qualities about him, André was wise beyond his years, Rhyse — well, Rhyse was in a class of his own, a dick who knew his worth and flaunted it. At least, that was how Thomas saw him. Perhaps that would change over time, once he got to know Rhyse better. But until then, Thomas was quite happy calling him a dick in his head. *Because he kind of is one.*

Regardless, Thomas missed conversing with these intelligent men who wanted him as part of their own. He had a feeling they wouldn't be offering this opportunity to just anyone.

Once back home, he walked into an empty apartment. The plate he'd left for Gunter was clean and drying on the counter. *That was thoughtful of him. Though, I'm sure he thought the same of me leaving it out for him. I hope so.*

This hope sparked something within Thomas. He knew deep down that change was hard for him. That was why he was weighing these new opportunities so heavily. As he played his James Tyler record, he decided to take the chance on the pack — and Gunter. He'd spent the majority of his life alone, and he felt he was ready to open himself up to others.

*Because what else will you do otherwise? Continue living a detached existence by yourself? With no one to comfort you when you're troubled and sad? With no one to help protect you, help you grow, and learn more about yourself. When else will you get this opportunity?*

James sang in the background while Thomas laid down on the couch. He stared at the ceiling as the music played, and soon nodded off.

*He dreamt about the end of the world again. But this time, Gunter was there, covered in his own blood and bleeding from an open wound on his arm. He extended his hand toward Thomas, crying out for help. The doll was there again, staring Thomas down with its lifeless sockets. The world around them crumbled, towering buildings falling, lightning striking the ground, the wind howling as it enveloped Thomas.*

He awoke as Gunter was screaming. His heart was racing, and sweat dripped down his face. He got this overwhelming sense to take care of Gunter, that he needed Thomas' help to heal. And Thomas wanted to be the one to heal him.

*Let Gunter in.*

He changed into his barista apparel and headed back to the coffee shop for his shift. He couldn't focus on the work or the customers. He messed up orders and listened while the customers angrily called him out. He mumbled half-assed apologies while he remade the drinks and refunded some of the snottier patrons.

By the time nine o'clock rolled around, and they closed their doors, he was antsy and ready to get the hell out. He wanted to see the pack again.

He bade goodbye to Shalese, who had more questions for him. He said that he had to get going after she offered to sit down and chat. She understood and let him go.

Thomas promised her that he would text her soon, and that he'd be back tomorrow night for his next shift.

Then he made his way to Moore's Forest, shifting once he was far enough away from the highway, and let the night take him away.

"Thomas!" André exclaimed as they greeted each other in the castle courtyard. Gunter was standing behind him, smiling at Thomas.

"I'm glad you made it back," Gunter said.

"Me too. André, if the offer still stands, I'd like to accept your invitation to join the pack."

André clasped his hands together. "Splendid!" he exclaimed. "What made you accept?"

Thomas shrugged. "I have nothing going for myself right now, I'm just existing. I want to belong to something. Something bigger than myself."

"That's a wonderful answer," André said.

Just then, Rhyse materialized out of nowhere and walked up to them. "André, I need to talk to you. Now," he said urgently.

"What is it?" André asked.

Rhyse glared at Thomas, then looked back at André. "Inside."

"Very well. Apologies, Thomas."

"No worries. Can we chat?" Thomas asked Gunter.

"Of course," Gunter said. "Let's go to the bedroom."

"Perfect." He gave André a nod and said, "I'll come back to talk to you soon."

"Take your time, gentlemen," said André, and the four of them left the courtyard and headed into the castle.

Thomas followed Gunter through the winding hallways and up a set of stairs to the hall on the second floor.

"Should we sit?" Gunter said, gesturing to the bed.

Thomas sat and patted the bedspread. Gunter smiled and took a seat next to him.

"So what's on your mind, Thomas?" he asked.

"I do want to join the pack, but I don't know if I'm willing to give myself to someone else quite yet. I'm still reeling from the events surrounding Jonathan, and I need to sort out my feelings. Actually, I need to *find* Jonathan. Before I can even begin to..." He trailed off, staring blankly at the stained-glass window.

"I understand. I, myself, am not quite prepared for a new relationship. Why don't we take it slow? One step at a time, no?"

Thomas grinned. "Yeah. I like that idea."

"Good. Me, too."

Thomas studied Gunter's warm brown eyes. He looked back at Thomas with as much sincerity and curiosity.

"You're truly breathtaking," Gunter whispered.

Thomas laughed. "Me?" He inched closer. "What about *you*?"

They stared at each other for a long moment, then when Thomas tried to kiss Gunter, he pulled away.

"I'm sorry," Gunter said.

"Don't be. Hey," Thomas said, reaching for Gunter's hand. "One step at a time, right?"

Gunter smiled. "One step at a time."

\* \* \* \*

André sat at the desk in his study, old books scattered across the surface. The room smelled of used, loved books — that strong, calming scent that André adored so much. *Smells like knowledge*, he mused.

He lifted his gaze from the book he had open in front of him to Rhyse, standing with his hands behind his back.

"This shapeshifter you're so willing to accept into our pack..." Rhyse began. "You don't know what you're getting yourself wrapped up in. *All* of us. The repercussions will be dire."

"For whom? In what way?" André asked.

"For all of us, André. There are others out there seeking him. They want him. For what, I don't know."

"Who is looking for him?"

Rhyse inhaled and closed his eyes. Then he opened them and stared down André. "Andromeda," he said grimly.

"Andromeda wouldn't *dare* return to us. Not after what happened last time."

"She escaped with her life, yes, and there were casualties. But don't for a second think that she is still wounded — she has healed herself."

"Vampires cannot heal themselves," André said. "They carry their wounds for the rest of their miserable lives."

"But she can. She has found a way."

"How?"

Rhyse looked away. "I cannot say."

André sighed. "Damn it, Rhyse, how can I lead my pack if I am not prepared for what lies ahead?"

"You know what information can do to the future. It can change it, it can — "

"It should be changed, Rhyse."

"It should *not* be changed. The very fabric of time itself could be altered in an irreversible way — "

"Then enlighten me, Griesbach!"

Rhyse backed down, softening his stance.

André went on. "*Enlighten me!* Tell me why you disclosing the future could damage everything around us."

Rhyse took a breath. "As you wish."

He took André's hand and closed his eyes.

André flew back in his chair. He was surrounded by stars swirling around him, and he could see planets revolving around them as they rushed by. He saw the end of the world — or rather, the end of everything. He saw the universe implode on itself, all the stars dying one by one. Planets began to spin freely in outer space, then he saw Earth — it passed by him in a blur — and he heard the screams of billions of people in limbo.

He retracted his hand and rubbed it, then he gaped in awe at Rhyse.

"How did you do that?"

"I can show others what I see if I so choose."

"Why did you never disclose this to me?!" André shouted. "What faith can I put in you to protect my pack if you keep these things from me?"

"You've just seen the end of not just the world, but the whole universe. This is what will happen if I reveal too much. The fabric of time is a thin strand, and it can be easily broken by those who possess such a power to break it. I shouldn't have even showed you that. Just...trust me."

"Hard to do when you keep things from me!"

Rhyse sighed. "I need to go meditate. I need to see what Andromeda is planning, and when she's coming. We need to be ready. Do you not remember her foreboding words on the rooftop of that movie theater? I told you that night that she was after someone — I just hadn't known who. But now I do. She's after Thomas, and nothing we do will stop her. We need to convene and come up with a plan of attack, and Thomas needs to go back to where he came from."

"No, we need to protect Thomas — he is too valuable an asset to let him walk away!"

"The vampires will stop at nothing to fulfill their destiny, and they will slaughter us all."

"Then we will fight!" André declared.

"If we fight, we will lose. I have seen it. A bloodbath. All our pack members dead, the pups dead, *you* dead."

André sighed and sat back in his chair. "This is highly frustrating. I hope you realize. Do me a favor, Rhyse, and tell me what their destiny is. What do the vampires want?"

Rhyse pursed his lips. "You're not going to let me go with this one, are you?"

André stood up, palms on the desk. He glared at Rhyse. "Tell me, or you're out of the pack."

"You don't want to do that. You can't afford to do that."

"You don't know what I can afford to do. Now, *tell me.*"

André watched as Rhyse deliberated for a moment. "You're putting me in an awful position here. I can't—"

"You will! Or you will leave."

Rhyse bit his lip. "So be it…Andromeda will not rest until all lycans are dead, and all shapeshifters captured."

"But why? To what end?"

Rhyse shrugged. "I can't tell you that. Only she can."

With that, he left André alone to wallow in his thoughts.

\* \* \* \*

Rhyse sat in the courtyard cross-legged in a meditation pose, his eyes shut. The leaves of the trees around him sang their lively songs as they shuddered in the wind.

In his mind, he was watching the path of a Nightstalker wandering the cold, dark streets of downtown Creston Bay. The vampire was admiring a youthful boy with pouty lips and long, straight black hair. The boy was entering a club with a girl on his arm.

The vampire stalked into the club behind them on quiet feet with hunger on his lips.

The vampire snarled and licked his slimy teeth with a slithering red tongue.

Rhyse recognized at once who he was watching.

"So," he said to himself, his words masked by the gentle breeze of wind. "You have found me at last."

Just then, André came into the courtyard and stood next to Rhyse. He cleared his throat and Rhyse opened his eyes.

"What can you see?" André asked.

"They are getting closer. One of them—the man I recognize—is stopping at a nightclub downtown to feed. Then I assume they'll make their way south to us. He knows I'm watching his movements. As such, he's stayed quiet. I can't seem to find the others...only him."

"Who is he?" André asked.

Rhyse sighed. "An estranged lover."

"I'm going to get Gunter."

"No," Rhyse objected. It was quick and irreverent.

"Rhyse, we need to be prepared. We need all pack members here to defend the castle."

"You do not see what I see."

"No, you're right. I don't," André said, still fired up from their argument. "But Gunter knows more about them than I do. We could use him."

"And what about Thomas? Surely if Gunter comes, Thomas will follow. And then what? Should we be responsible for an inexperienced shifter—who, I might add, is not yet a member of this pack?"

André sucked in a breath and cracked his neck. "I'm getting Gunter and that's final."

"What good am I to you if you do not listen?"

André walked back into the castle without another word.

* * * *

Gunter and Thomas had spent the last hour talking about everything from religion to politics and climate change, learning more about each other as time passed. Gunter feared for the future of Mother Earth, Thomas feared for the future of humanity and what this all meant. They had discussed likes and dislikes, mannerisms they had, mannerisms they'd noticed in each other...it had been a fruitful conversation, and Thomas had loved every minute of it.

This man was intoxicating, lighting a fire within Thomas, and he loved it. It excited him, made him feel alive. He wanted to know everything about Gunter.

Mid-conversation, someone knocked at the door. "Come in," Thomas called.

André entered the room with a serious expression on his face. "We need to prepare for battle. The vampires are approaching."

"What do they want?" Gunter asked.

André looked at Thomas then back at Gunter.

"Why?" said Gunter.

"They have a keen fascination with shapeshifters, and they won't rest until they find him."

Gunter looked at Thomas, concern plastered across his face. "You need to stay here."

"What? Why?" Thomas said.

"Because you're not ready for this, Thomas," said André. "Nightstalkers are nasty creatures who revel in chaos."

"But if they're after me, should I not be included? What if they slaughter you guys?"

"That's a risk we're willing to take, Thomas," said André. "But we are not willing to risk losing you. You're too valuable."

"I see," Thomas said quietly, pondering this. "What can I do to help?"

"Stay here," Gunter said. "Trust me, we'll take care of it. I promise."

"But I don't want to lose you. Any of you! I want to help in any way I can."

"You can help us by staying here," André said.

Thomas thought for a moment. "This doesn't sit well with me. The vampires are here for me, and you guys are willing to potentially walk into a bloodbath for me?"

"Thomas, you are special. You are gifted," said André. "And we need you more than ever right now. But you're not quite ready for battle—have you ever met a Nightstalker?"

"At Jonathan's condo, yeah."

"They're foul creatures who seek only to destroy."

Thomas remembered his conversation with Shalese earlier today—how she said vampires weren't all bad. He wondered if these Nightstalkers could be swayed somehow.

"I want to help."

"Please, Thomas, if you want to help us, you will stay here," Gunter said.

"We don't have much time," André said to Gunter. "We need to go. Now."

Thomas and Gunter stood. Gunter took Thomas' hands and said, "I'll come back for you."

"Promise?"

"Promise."

Thomas pulled him in for a hug. "Please don't die."

Gunter chuckled. "You doubt my skills, Thomas. I'm very well-versed in this sort of thing."

"Okay," said Thomas. "I trust you."

"Good. I'll return soon. Stay. Here. Please," Gunter pleaded.

"I will."

With that, Gunter and André exited the bedroom, and Thomas was left feeling anxious and small.

\* \* \* \*

Outside in the courtyard, André was preparing his council, trying to remain calm.

"What are we gonna do?" Rowtag asked. His anxiety was thick in his shaking voice—he'd never battled a Nightstalker before.

"We're going to stand our ground," André stated. "The last thing we want to do is appear as a threat to them without first understanding the context. We must be poised and collected, but prepared. As you all know, a Nightstalker is one of the most hostile creatures on this planet—more so than our own kind."

"Are we ready?" Rhyse asked.

"My chain-of-command will follow me out. The rest of you," he said, addressing the pups, "stay here. Come out only if a fight is imminent."

"But we want to help!" Max exclaimed. "We're not scared of a coven of vampires."

"Stay inside. Please," André said. "We can't afford to lose everyone. We will go out and address them, and should we need you, we'll call you in. Remain in the courtyard and keep a weather eye."

The pack nodded in unison and Rowtag, Gunter, Rhyse and Krister followed André out through the courtyard, over the drawbridge and into the dark woods beyond the castle.

# Chapter Seven

## Andromeda

The Nightstalkers emerged from a light fog that had started drifting through the woods. The moon above them waned in the night sky, the stars hidden behind thin clouds. There was a breeze that grew stronger with each gust, and it ravaged the waves from the lake as they kicked up against the shore.

There were four of them, tall, sickly thin and even paler than the moon, and they stalked closer with grace. Their faces were contorted into odd angular shapes from the curse of vampirism. Their skin was folded up to their cheekbones and all four of them wore a grotesque and horrifying smirk from one side of their faces to the other. None of them had a single hair on their heads, their noses had been reduced to slits for nostrils, and those eyes...those menacing, preternatural red eyes that glowed even in the darkest patch of trees stared down the lycans with a twisted look of excitement.

When they had come close enough to talk, they stopped. Their uniform black capes swayed in the wind.

The one on the far left spoke first. "So nice to see you were expecting us," he hissed through his two sharp, needle-like fangs. He looked straight at Rhyse. "Well done, my friend."

"That's your estranged lover?" André whispered to Rhyse.

"He looked much more charming when he was feeding on animals," Rhyse replied. Then, to the Nightstalker, he said, "I can say it's a surprise to see you here, Caston. Why have you come?"

"You know why I'm here." Caston stared Rhyse down with fiery eyes that alternated between a deep maroon and burnt orange like two colors inside a lava lamp.

"He's not here, if that's what you're getting at," Rhyse said.

"Ah, but we have a Foresight of our own—lovely Miss Andromeda Q'Ali Demire Jocasta II. You might have heard of her."

"The second Nightstalker queen," André said to Rowtag and Krister, who both looked lost.

"Her gifts, however, are far more powerful than your own, Rhyse Griesbach."

"You are afraid," Andromeda said. It was so soft and poetic that it sounded like a hymn. She was addressing Rowtag, who was shaking and gripping his arms.

Rowtag shook his head. "Just a little cold."

"You are afraid and angry, because you harbor a strong hatred toward our kind. But you are also naïve, and young and foolish. You should not bear your emotions on your sleeve like you do. It can get you killed."

Andromeda's eyes flared a bright green, and Rowtag fell to the ground, screaming in agony. His eyes bulged and he writhed on the grass, clawing at his scalp.

"Stop!" André commanded. "Stop it now!"

Andromeda sneered, and Caston laughed to himself. Then he asked, "Why would you appoint such a youngling as part of your chain-of-command?"

André responded, "He is young, but he is also wise and resourceful! Leave him be, Andromeda!"

The desperate cries from Rowtag ceased, and he stopped shaking. He grasped his head in his palm and slowly stood on his feet. Then he looked at Andromeda and shouted, "You fucking twat!"

The four Nightstalkers hissed.

"She got inside my head," Rowtag said. "She saw my past, my secrets. She saw my little sister and my mother get murdered by my father. She saw me eat that homeless man. She saw *everything*."

"Did you know that your father enjoyed being a murderer?" Andromeda said.

"Shut up!" Rowtag shouted, pointing a finger at her. "You just shut the fuck up! You don't know me!"

Then Andromeda's eyes sparkled again, and she said, "Aha! The boy is here — in the castle."

\* \* \* \*

Thomas paced around the room, gripping his head as his mind dizzied him. "Fuck," he swore. "Fuck! Shit."

Just then, a knock came at the door. "Yeah," Thomas said.

In came Max, confident and poised for a sixteen-year-old. "You want to help them, don't you?"

"Yeah, I do..."

"I think I can help you get to them without them noticing."

"You can? How?"

Max grinned and sat down on the bed. Thomas sat as well.

"I can get you out there. You can shift into something small, like a squirrel, right?"

Thomas nodded.

"Good, because we'll need to be discreet. If André knew I led you to them, he'd banish me from the pack, I'm sure."

"We? What do you mean?" Thomas asked.

Max's face lit up, and he stood in front of Thomas. Then, Max shifted into not a lycan but a Northern cardinal. He flitted above Thomas for a minute then shifted back.

"Ta-da!" Max said, spreading his arms.

Thomas smiled. "I think André would banish you if he knew you were a shapeshifter all this time and didn't tell him."

Max rolled his eyes. "Ugh, André and his obsession with shapeshifters. It's excessive, honestly. I didn't want to be poked and prodded and studied like a test subject of his. Plus, I know why the Nightstalkers are here. I've been hiding in this castle, away from them, for the past couple years."

"What do they want?"

"They want—*Andromeda* wants to suck the life force out of shapeshifters to absorb their power."

"How do you know this?"

Max shrugged. "I just do."

"No, you found out about this somehow," Thomas said.

Max rolled his eyes in a teenager-y way that Thomas found annoying. "I was captured. But I escaped."

"You got captured by Nightstalkers?"

"Yeah. It was the scariest shit I've ever gone through in my life. I escaped, but they think I'm dead. I almost was."

"Fuck. Are you talking about *these* Nightstalkers?"

Max nodded.

"Max, you can't go out there. If they see you—"

"They won't see me, I promise. They won't even see you, as long as you stay hidden."

\* \* \* \*

Gunter, standing next to André, assessed his unwanted guests, thinking of Thomas in that bedroom, waiting for him.

"Where is the boy?" Caston said.

Andromeda raised a hand at him for silence. "The boy is all we have come for. Surrender him and we'll leave you in peace." She said it condescendingly, as if she were addressing a child.

"What boy?" Gunter asked.

"The shapeshifter," Caston said. "He's here. Just bring him to us and this'll all be over."

"He won't be able to hide for long," the Nightstalker next to Andromeda said. "I'll find him."

From far up in a nearby tree, Thomas pricked his little squirrel ears up. Something about the voice of that Nightstalker just now...

The Nightstalker went on, "I know Thomas, and he's not one to cower. If you won't take us to him, I'll just have to kill you all."

Thomas leapt out of the tree and shifted mid-air back into his human form. He landed firmly on the balls of his feet. Slowly, he stood up straight and approached the Nightstalker. He stared him down for a moment, and when he was sure of it, he gasped.

"Jonathan."

"Hey, you piece of shit," Jonathan spat. "I've been looking for you."

Thomas gawked at the sight of his former lover, this pasty white being with a scowl on his face and his head bare. Jonathan wasn't a man anymore. He wasn't a lycan, either. He was a monster.

"It was you," Thomas said with a twinge of shock "In your condo earlier. That was *you*."

Jonathan chuckled. "You didn't recognize me?"

"Hey, I was worried about you!" Thomas yelled.

"Worried about me? That's rich."

"Jonathan," Thomas said with a sigh, "I'm sorry, I didn't know that I'd turn you — "

"Don't be sorry. You've given me an infinite power — power I never dreamt I could have."

Jonathan stepped closer to Thomas and snarled through razor-sharp fangs. Then he shifted into a lycan, his beast of large and mighty stature with thick black fur and menacing emerald eyes. He charged at Thomas, who for a moment was horrorstruck. Rowtag shifted into his wolf and intercepted Jonathan, tackling him to the ground. Jonathan growled and shifted again, this time into a python, and wrapped his brown spotted body around Rowtag's wolf form. Jonathan tightened his grip and squeezed, and Rowtag let out a yelp as he writhed on the ground.

"Let him go!" Thomas cried. "This is our fight, Jonathan!"

Jonathan's python head hissed at Thomas while his body tightened even further on Rowtag's ribcage. A loud *crack!* resounded and sleeping birds awoke with a fright and fled their nests. Rowtag yelped again, this sound much weaker than the first.

Thomas leapt into the air and shifted into a black panther, claws out and teeth bared. Jonathan unwound himself from Rowtag, who had fallen to the ground in defeat, and shifted himself into his wolf once more. They met in the middle, and Thomas slashed Jonathan's face, spraying blood on the dirt. Angered, Jonathan roared, and the other pack members shifted into their own supernatural forms. They swarmed in on Thomas and Jonathan but were impeded by the three Nightstalkers.

After dodging Jonathan's novice combat moves, Thomas got scratched by his thick claws. He retreated a few steps back and shifted into his human form again to speak.

"Are those the only three things you've learned to transform into?" Thomas said with a mocking tone.

Jonathan became human and responded, "They're all I need to kill you."

"Why kill me, Jonathan? Why join them? They don't know what it's like to be a shapeshifter. Come with us, and we'll make you stronger than you'd ever believe you could be."

"You stupid fuck, don't you know I *am* the strongest I'll ever be? And these vampires know everything about shapeshifters. Come — join *us*, Thomas. You don't have to be alone anymore. You can be part of a family. The strongest, most resilient family in all of history."

The Nightstalkers stopped in their tracks and shifted their focus to Jonathan and Thomas a few yards closer to the cliff. The lycans stopped, following their gazes, and listening to what the two were arguing about.

"Like hell I'd join you," Thomas spat. "And what are you talking about? I changed you because I was in lycan form, and it was a full moon."

"The shapeshifting ability cannot be transferred or given to a mortal who does not possess the dormant trait," the Nightstalker Andromeda said, stepping closer to them.

The lycans stayed poised to fight, but off to the side awaiting an attack.

"Dormant...?" Thomas muttered to himself.

"Jonathan possesses unspeakable power within him," Andromeda said. "This power has been inside him all along, but your touch ignited the flame that transformed him."

"All right..." Thomas shook his head. "Enough. Why did he assume the form of a lycan?" he asked Andromeda, who was staring him down like a piece of meat.

"He made physical contact with you," she answered. "The power of the full moon aided that."

"A shapeshifter mimics what it touches," Caston said in his slithery voice. "The subject's DNA is absorbed through the skin. All of its DNA."

"This means Thomas does have the Z chromosome," André declared. "You *are* part lycan. And part shapeshifter. And part human. You are —"

"A hybrid," Andromeda said. "Just like our Jonathan."

"You know, Thomas, I guess I should be thanking you," Jonathan said. "You've awoken something in me that's more valuable than all the money in the damn world. And these vampires have given me an even more powerful gift than you could give me — the gift of vampirism."

"And you, Thomas, have delivered us something extremely useful — an invaluable asset," Caston said, stepping forward. "You see, when dear Jonathan here stumbled across our hideout, a scared and trembling lycan, we saw an opportunity. Allow me to show you." He grabbed Jonathan by the head and exposed his neck, then bit him and drank his blood. His eyes turned emerald, and he gave Thomas a sinister grin, licking his bloody teeth. He gave a preternatural growl and charged toward Thomas.

André intercepted the Nightstalker and ripped his arm clean off his shoulder. Caston screamed briefly and tumbled to the ground. But instead of writhing in pain, he stood up and laughed as his arm grew back.

André gasped. "The blood of a hybrid — "

"The One True Power," Andromeda said. "The Elixir of Life. The crème de la crème. The delectable blood of this hybrid makes us impervious to every possible death — even at the hands of a lycan."

"So you want to milk these poor boys for your Elixir of Life?" Rowtag exclaimed through grunts, easing himself up off the ground and gripping his side. "So you can, what, eradicate us lycans? Can't share the world, you have to have it all to your goddamned selves, is that it?"

"Shut up, Rowtag," Rhyse hissed from behind.

Rowtag pushed onward. "You can take Jonathan. I don't give a shit. But if you want Thomas, you'll have to go through me."

"Through all of us," André said, spreading his arms and gesturing for the lycans to flock beside him.

"You think we want this one?" Caston said with a sneer. "You're so ill-informed, André."

"What—?"

"He doesn't know," Andromeda said to Caston.

Caston grinned. "Even better."

Caston eyed the forest, looking once at Thomas, then to the cardinal perched on a branch above.

"No!" Thomas cried.

Max shifted into his lycan and pounced on Caston. What ensued next was a bloodbath—Max destroyed Caston, ripping him limb from limb and gnawing at his insides. The *crunch* of Caston's bones sent shivers through Thomas. He looked to Andromeda, who was clearly frightened now. Off came Caston's head, and Max flung it toward Andromeda. She screamed in anger. Caston's blank expression stared at her, and she hissed at Max. She charged toward him, but André intercepted her and threw her to the ground with a *smack!* The unnamed Nightstalkers attacked Rhyse, who skirted around him in lycan form like he was born to fight. Krister fought alongside André, clawing at Andromeda.

Jonathan ran toward Thomas, who crashed into Jonathan and pinned him to the ground.

"Don't do this, Jonathan!" Thomas shouted. "You can end this right now! Leave them!"

"You're such a simpleton, Thomas." Then Jonathan shifted into his python again and attempted to wrap himself around Thomas—but Thomas would not let him. He shifted into a lycan and attacked Jonathan, slashing at him with his claws.

Gunter swooped in and aided Thomas. The three of them fought while the rest of the pack assaulted the Nightstalkers. Max shifted back into human form, exhausted and dripping with blood. What remained of Caston's body was a bloody, gelatinous mass that was desperately trying to heal itself. It wriggled on the ground.

"Caston!" Andromeda cried, reaching for the remains. André ripped her arm clean off. Blood sprayed the grass. She turned back to André, who had her pinned down.

Then Andromeda's body disintegrated into a plume of black dust, freeing her from Thomas and André. The dust rose to the sky, hovered fifteen feet above the ground, then collected to form Andromeda's body. She floated there for a moment, then shrieked. Her mouth dropped, and her eyes turned black.

Andromeda extended her arms and fire shot from her hands. She spread the fire across the trees, and they lit up, burning in the night. Her screams continued.

"*Andromeda!*" André shouted. "*Stop it now!*"

She started to cackle like a witch, her black eyes staring down at the lycans as they watched in horror, the trees blazing around them.

Thomas shifted into an eagle, swooped up into the air and slashed Andromeda's throat with his talons. She fell to the ground, landing on her heels. Her throat healed itself as quickly as it was sliced open.

She approached André, bloodlust in her eyes. Her mouth dripped with saliva and her slimy red tongue slithered between her fangs.

"No!" Max cried and ran toward her.

She looked right at him as he charged — then a look of shock crossed her face. Her expression changed to delight.

"There you are...come."

Max looked at André, who looked back at him, bewildered. "You—?"

"André, I—"

Andromeda snapped her fingers. The fighting stopped abruptly as the Nightstalkers looked at her. She ignored their gazes and sauntered toward Max, fire once more shooting from her palms. The lycans ran toward her and André intercepted her, tackling her to the ground. With one swift motion, she gripped his head and twisted it. In one quick *snap!* André's neck went limp, and his body fell to the ground.

Gunter shifted back into his human form. "*André!*" he screamed. "*Nooooo!*"

Andromeda's cackle resounded throughout the forest, crystal-clear in the cacophony of burning trees and raging winds.

Rhyse shifted again and charged toward her, the rest of the lycans following. But they were too far away — she reached Max before them, grabbed him by the waist, and burst into dust again, disappearing into the air.

Max was gone.

# Chapter Eight

## One of the Pack

The newscaster rambled on about the ongoing fire in Moore's Forest. In the bar, a man watched the TV while he sipped a rum and cola.

"Such a shame, isn't it?" the girl next to him said.

"It's the fuckin' vamps that did it," the man replied. "This has their name written all over it."

"How do you know that?"

He shrugged. "Just a feeling." His attention went back to the TV.

The newscaster said to his correspondent, "Ashley, what's going on down there?"

The shot cut to Ashley Whittaker, reporter for Fox 11 News. The banner at the bottom of the screen read "Fire Destroys Moore's Forest—Vampires to Blame?"

"Ron, I'm reporting to you from the edge of Moore's Forest, where a fire is ravaging the beloved island. The smoke is so bad that it's difficult to breathe. The sky is bright orange, and the flames are engulfing the whole forest. We don't know what caused the fire yet, but reports from passersby on the highway said they saw a vampire hovering in the air at the time the fire started."

"Hey man, can you change the channel to sports or sumthin?" the man said to the bartender.

The bartender switched the channel. On came CNN—an anchor was interviewing a Republican congressional candidate.

"Now Robert, you say that vampires are behind the fires in Moore's Forest—what does this mean for vampires' rights? What does this mean for the vampire movement and hashtag-vampires-were-human-once?"

"Well, the implications are dire for the undead, Anderson. This display of power is shocking, and we have to wonder what else they can do. What else are vampires capable of that we don't even know? This doesn't look good for the vampires' rights movement."

"Hey, buddy," the man said to the bartender, "that's not fuckin' sports."

"Shhh!" the girl hushed.

Robert the congressional candidate continued, "The general public does not look kindly on vampires, and distrust is still there, and frankly, Anderson, I don't think—um, this just doesn't bode well for the vampires and—"

The anchor cut him off and said, "Robert, your platform is based on this—well, I'm gonna say 'conspiracy theory,' that vampires want to turn all humans and enslave them—"

"It's not a conspiracy, Anderson, they are plotting this already, facts have been proven about it and—"

"Robert, you say in your campaign rallies that vampires are selfish and self-serving. Can't the same be said about us? About human beings?"

* * * *

In the lower level of the castle, Thomas and the pack surrounded a casket. André's body rested inside, hands posed on his chest and his eyes closed. Thomas was choking back tears. He noticed Rhyse was staring at André's body with a blank expression — no emotion, no sadness. It was peculiar...*too* peculiar.

"Did you know?" Thomas asked him.

He looked up. "Did I know what?"

Thomas took a step closer. "Did you know that André was going to die?"

The pack looked at Rhyse, who seemed defensive. "The sands of time reveal all. I can only see what is given to me."

"Did...you...*know*?"

Rhyse sighed. "Yes."

"And you didn't tell us?!" Rowtag exclaimed. "How fucking *dare* you?"

"If I told you all that André was going to die tonight, what would you have done differently?" Rhyse said.

"We would have been prepared," Thomas said. "We would have been ready. We would have fought with all we had, not once let our guard down. Or, maybe we would have kept André inside the castle. I don't know, but I *do* know that you're a fucking traitor, Rhyse!"

"Easy there, Thomas."

"No!" Thomas got in his face. "You fucked up royally. You were complicit in the murder of your own leader. Fucking despicable. Did you let him die? Did you intentionally not protect him so that he would meet his fate?"

Rhyse bit his lip. "If I disrupt what time has in store for us, it could cause — "

"Oh, fuck your fucking excuses, Rhyse!" Rowtag shouted. "I'm so sick of you using that rhetoric to absolve yourself of your actions! Thomas is right, you were complicit. You're a traitor, and you should be banished."

"You can't banish me, Rowtag," Rhyse said snidely. "I'm taking over the pack, and you will follow my orders. If you refuse, *you* will be banished."

"You fucking slimeball—!"

"Rowtag!" Gunter said. "Hush. Rhyse, André informed me before the battle that should he die, Thomas was to take over the pack."

Rhyse scoffed. "You think I'm going to believe that?"

"It doesn't matter if *you* believe it—the question is, does everyone else believe it?"

"All in favor of Thomas being the pack leader?" Rowtag said.

Every single member raised their hand, except for Rhyse and Krister.

"Krister?" Rhyse said.

Krister reservedly looked at Rhyse. "You had a hand in André's death. You should be banished. But Thomas should not be the pack leader. He's too inexperienced. It should be me."

"Well, still looks like you're outnumbered, Krister," said Rowtag. "So...eat shit and leave."

Krister gritted his teeth. "Just try and banish me, Rowtag. I dare you."

"Fine. All in favor of banishing this tool?"

Everyone but Rhyse raised their hands. Krister scowled at the rest of them like they were filth. "All right then. Fuck you all, too." Then he left without another word.

"Now...*you*," Thomas said to Rhyse. "You get the fuck out, too."

Rhyse looked at the rest of the pack, and they returned his gaze with expressions of anger.

"So be it," Rhyse said. Then he left up the stone stairs to the main level and walked out of the castle.

Thomas remained with Gunter, Rowtag and the pups. They spent hours in that room, mourning the loss of a great leader.

"André would have wanted us to keep him here," Gunter said. "This castle was all he had left of his family. It belonged to his great-grandfather, Marcus, who had it built for his wife. Amelia's Stronghold, it was called. Once André had inherited the castle, he changed the name to Bramwell, after his lover, Everett Bramwell, who had died in a tragic train crash. This castle was his home and had been for almost one hundred years. He would want to be kept down here, at the lowest part of the castle, to rest for eternity. It is here he shall lay. Rest in peace, our dear friend."

They cried in unison while the casket was closed. They each placed a single white rose on top.

"Rest in peace, André," Rowtag said, resting his palm on the casket. A tear trickled down his cheek. "I'll take good care of the pups for you. I'll find Max. And Andromeda will pay."

All but Thomas and Gunter went up the stairs to the main level. Gunter took Thomas' hand.

"Ready?" Gunter asked.

"Hold on. I want a moment alone with André."

"Of course." Gunter exited the room.

Thomas turned to the casket once more. "Thank you for giving me this opportunity, André. I'll never forget you." He began to cry. "I'll protect them. I promise."

Thomas stood there for a few minutes in silence. He knew André was in a better place now. He didn't believe in much, but he did believe in an afterlife. *And André is there, looking down on you. He'll continue to guide you. You're not alone in this...*

\* \* \* \*

Thomas emerged from the lower floor with puffy red eyes. Gunter was waiting for him under an archway leading to the great hall. They walked through the winding hallways and up several sets of stairs to the study. Thomas sat in André's chair and admired his new friends — his new pack.

*My new pack...this can't be. How am I the one in André's chair? Why not Rowtag? Why not Gunter? Why me, André?*

"How is it that you all trust me to be your leader?" he asked the room.

Rowtag shrugged. "You were obviously very important to André, and he trusted you. So we trust you, too."

"You all feel this way?"

They nodded.

"I can't believe this. All my life I've felt alone. Misunderstood. Ignored. But here, I feel like I belong. Like I'm where I need to be. I don't know why that is — probably because you're all so welcoming and kind to me. And trusting of me, too, which is...nice. I'm glad that those who were untrusting of me are gone now."

"Me, too," said Alejandro. "They were dicks." Thomas could tell he was broken up about Max's disappearance — it was in his tone. Thomas felt for the boy and thought back to Gunter's story of his first boyfriend — how swiftly things changed.

"Yeah, they kind of were," Thomas said with a small chuckle to lighten the mood a bit. "So where does this leave us?"

"We were hoping you'd know the answer to that," Rowtag said.

"Well, I don't. I can't even fathom being a leader of anything, let alone the leader of a pack of lycans."

"Don't worry, I'll help you find your footing," said Gunter.

"Thank you, I'd appreciate that, Gunter. Rowtag, why don't you take the pups to bed?"

"Sure thing, alpha." He gave Thomas a wink.

"All right, then, off you go," said Thomas with a smile.

Rowtag and the pups exited the room, leaving Gunter alone with Thomas.

"I'm so tired," Thomas said with a yawn.

"I'll take you to your room, then," Gunter replied.

\* \* \* \*

Gunter shut the door behind him as he entered the bedroom.

"Will you stay with me?" Thomas asked Gunter.

"Of course."

Thomas got under the covers. "Come here."

Gunter obeyed and lay next to him. He wrapped an arm gently around Thomas.

"I'm not sure how you're feeling about this all, but...I'm ready."

"Ready?" Gunter said.

"Yeah, I'm ready to love you. I want you. I want to be close to you. Are you ready?"

Gunter smiled. "I'm ready, dear Thomas."

Gunter leaned in for a kiss, and Thomas kissed him back with all the passion he'd had building up inside. Gunter's lips were so soft, so inviting. And his body was so warm.

Thomas pulled away to whisper, "Take me."

Thomas was overcome with arousal when Gunter's growing member pressed against his thigh. Sensually, he kissed his way down Thomas' neck and caressed his body. Thomas' cock was throbbing with anticipation. He felt Gunter's beard on his skin, and it made precum drip from his dick. He moaned when Gunter playfully licked his nipple.

He closed his eyes as Gunter went down on him, taking his whole cock in his mouth. The pleasure was overwhelming, and Thomas' breathing accelerated. His body was aflame, burning hot and sweating.

"Fuck." He exhaled. He ran his fingers through Gunter's hair while his cock was sucked.

Gunter used his tongue to tease the head of Thomas' cock, gave it another sensual lick down the shaft, and sucked on Thomas' balls.

"Oh...!" Thomas groaned. "Fuck, you're good at that."

Gunter chuckled.

Thomas opened his eyes and watched Gunter suck his dick. Gunter looked up at him with his big brown eyes and released his cock, then rose up to give Thomas a wet kiss.

"Fuck me," Thomas whispered.

"You sure?" Gunter asked.

Thomas nodded. "Yeah. I need you."

Gunter kissed him again, then trailed his tongue down Thomas' torso, licking the grooves in his abdomen, giving his cock another suck, then he pulled Thomas closer to him and licked his hole.

Thomas inhaled. "Ohhhh, fuck."

Gunter continued to rim Thomas and guided his index finger inside. Thomas felt a pulse of ecstasy. He writhed in Gunter's gentle grasp.

"Right now."

"I don't have any lube," Gunter said.

Thomas sat up and reached for Gunter's cock. It was quite large, and for a second he worried he wouldn't be able to take it. Nonetheless, he sucked Gunter's cock, wetting it for what was to come. He heard Gunter growl in response.

"There. Now fuck me."

"You're sure?" Gunter asked.

"Yes, absolutely, yes."

"I'll start slow, promise."

Thomas nodded.

Then Gunter guided his cock into Thomas' hole. Thomas closed his eyes again and growled with pleasure. There was some pain, too, but it made the sex feel better. Once Gunter was all the way in, his balls grazing Thomas' cheeks, he leaned down for another kiss.

"You're so warm," he whispered.

"You're so *big*," Thomas said.

"Too big for you?"

"Not at all."

Gunter began thrusting, gently at first, but when Thomas commanded him to go faster, he obeyed. Gunter kissed Thomas' body everywhere he could reach while he drove his cock harder. Sweat dripped from Gunter's forehead and his breath was hot against Thomas' skin. Gunter worked Thomas' cock, jerking it up and down while he rammed into Thomas.

Thomas moaned with pleasure and his hole clenched around Gunter's cock. He was close already.

"Fuck, I'm almost there," Thomas said with a gasp. Gunter stopped. "What's wrong?"

"I want you to fuck me," Gunter breathed.

Thomas nearly came just hearing those words.

"You wanna have some fun with it?" Thomas said with a grin.

Gunter pulled out, his dick throbbing. "Sure."

Thomas shifted into Evan Winston, his dick growing from a modest girth to a larger, meatier size.

"Kiss me," Evan said in a sexy British accent that he could see drove Gunter wild.

"Holy fuck!" Gunter exclaimed. "You're fucking hot like this. I want you to fuck me then shift back while you're inside."

"Oh shit, okay," Evan said with a laugh. "Get on your hands and knees."

"Yes, sir," Gunter said. He did so, and Evan circled around to his backside. He ran his tongue up and down Gunter's spine, then down to his hole, teasing it, pleasuring it. He heard Gunter growl again, and it made his dick throb harder.

After a minute of rimming, he traced his tongue down to Gunter's balls and sucked hard.

Gunter let out a gasp. "Oof," he said. "That feels good."

Evan continued sucking, then fit both balls into his mouth.

"Fuck!" Gunter cried.

Evan let Gunter's balls loose and pulled his cock toward himself and sucked it. Gunter kept groaning. Evan wiggled a finger inside his ass, feeling a warm, wet sensation. Then, with one last suck on Gunter's balls, Evan went back up to his hole, gave it a final lick, then spat on his cock and guided it in.

Gunter said, "I want it rough. Fuck me raw."

Evan's whole body was on fire. His cock fit all the way in, his balls touching Gunter's. He ran his hand up and down Gunter's back, then gripped his hips and pounded him.

"Fuck! Harder!" Gunter nearly shouted.

Evan obeyed and repositioned himself. He pulled out then shoved back in, and Gunter resumed growling. Evan gave it his all, working his cock inside Gunter's ass. He reached around and jerked Gunter's dick while he thrust.

"Fuck, I'm gonna come—" Gunter said.

"Don't. Not yet."

Evan let go of his dick and shifted back into Thomas, continuing to push himself deep inside Gunter.

"That felt amazing," Gunter said.

"You want it rough?" Thomas breathed.

"Yes. Please."

Thomas shifted back into Evan, his dick growing in size once more, and Gunter let out a howl of pleasure.

"Fuck! Do that again!"

Evan shifted back into Thomas, thrust a few times, then shifted into Evan again.

"That feels so fucking good! Keep going!"

Thomas kept up this exercise, shifting back and forth between his alias and his true form, his dick growing and getting slightly smaller, then growing again.

But he, too, was getting close already. He pulled out. "Sorry," he said. "I got close."

"Don't worry, Thomas. Want to try something I'm sure you've never done before?" Gunter asked, panting.

"Oh yeah? What is it?"

Gunter grinned. "Fuck me in your wolf form."

Thomas' heart skipped a beat and his dick pulsed. *This man is so fucking hot.* "Are you sure?" he asked. "I'm pretty big as a wolf."

"I can take it. Promise."

Gunter buried his face into the pillow and arched his back, his ass to the ceiling, hole ready to receive Thomas' cock once more. *Just like a good bottom.*

Then Thomas slid his dick in and shifted.

His cock grew even more, thickening and extending further inside Gunter.

"Ohhh, fuck! Fuck!" Gunter shouted. "It's so good!"

Thomas' wolf put a paw on Gunter's back and thrust deep, pulled out, back in, pulled out, back in. He did this for what seemed like hours, Gunter moaning in ecstasy the whole time. The lycan leaned closer to Gunter's neck and gave him a satisfying lick.

"Do that again," Gunter said through the pillow.

Thomas went for his ear. Gunter moaned with pleasure.

Thomas was getting closer yet again. He was exhausted, and so he figured coming now was probably best. He was looking forward to the cuddling afterward.

The lycan's claws gripped Gunter's hips and pounded Gunter—faster and faster, until Thomas howled and shot his load deep within Gunter.

He shifted back into himself, gasping for air, and pulled out, his cum dripping from Gunter's hole. He then kissed the back of his neck.

"Fuck me again. Come all over me."

"As you wish," Gunter said.

Thomas lay down on his back, and Gunter lifted his legs up to his broad shoulders. Then Gunter slid his cock in, and Thomas closed his eyes. He bit his lip.

He put a hand on Gunter's chest. It didn't take long for Gunter to reach climax.

"Fuck, I'm gonna come," he gasped, and pulled out of Thomas. He worked his cock and sprayed strings of hot cum all over Thomas' chest. Still moaning, Gunter rested next to Thomas.

"That was the best sex I've ever had," Gunter said.

Thomas laughed. "I could say the same thing."

They kissed, and Gunter pressed his chest against Thomas, getting sticky with cum. The moon came out of the clouds just then and lit up the stained-glass window, spreading colors over their naked bodies.

\* \* \* \*

After the pups were asleep, Rowtag wandered outside and over the drawbridge. He looked around at the charred remains of Moore's Forest. He fought back tears as the reality of what had happened came flooding back.

*My leader is dead. My home is destroyed. Max has been kidnapped. What the fuck?*

"Where do we go from here, André?" he said to no one. "What's next?"

He looked up at the sky muddled with smoke from the fire, searching for an answer. "You guided me for the last six years. You taught me how to fight, how to defend—how to lead. I'll never forget you."

He closed his eyes and inhaled. A breeze raised goosebumps on his arms. The smell of ash filled his nostrils. He wept for André. He wept for the forest. He wept for everything they'd lost.

"I'll never let go of you," he whispered.

# Epilogue

The Archimedes Pack

Thomas awoke the next morning to rays of sun trickling in through the window. He yawned and sat up. Gunter was still fast asleep and snoring, which Thomas found cute.

He got up and dressed himself in a robe, then made his way to André's study — or, his study now. *God, that's weird. It's gonna take me a while to get used to this.*

There were stacks of books about shapeshifters on the desk, under the amber glow of a lamp. Spread across the surface of the desk was a large map of the world. Various regions were circled and there were names scribbled throughout. He took a seat and flipped through the pages of the book on the top of the stack. He stopped on a page that was highlighted.

*The shapeshifter almost always travels alone. Rarely do they let themselves be known, lest they be burned at the stake or stoned. Though, in some cases, shapeshifters have been known to hide among packs of lycanthropes, for they provide a sense of security and protection from those who wish shapeshifters harm.*

A note was jotted in pencil on the edge of the page, right next to the highlighted text. "Archimedes."

*Archimedes.* He'd seen that name written somewhere just earlier as he was looking around...

The map. He looked to North America and saw it — the upper peninsula of Michigan was circled and "Archimedes" was written next to it.

"André...you were looking for shapeshifters in other packs."

Just then, there was a knock at the door. "Enter," Thomas said.

In came Rowtag and Gunter.

"Ah, yes, my chain-of-command," Thomas said, clasping his hands together. He smiled at them.

"You sound just like André," Rowtag said with a grin.

"That's what I was going for. Look, I just found something."

The men approached him and looked over his shoulder as he pointed to the spot on the map.

"André was looking for shapeshifters in other packs of lycans," he said. "This one here, 'Archimedes'...I think that's a pack of lycans."

"What an odd name," Gunter mused. "Archimedes was an ancient Greek physicist. Why choose that name?"

"I guess we'll have to ask them," Thomas replied.

"Thomas, you're not thinking of pursuing this, are you?" Rowtag said with concern. "You don't want to attract vampires — "

"That's *exactly* what I want to do. I want to find other shapeshifters and build an alliance. I want enough in numbers to take down every last one of those fucking things. I want to avenge André's death. And I want

Andromeda to come to me. We find Andromeda, we find Max."

"I'll go with you," Gunter said.

"No...you need to stay here and guard the castle. Protect the pack, both of you. I'll go alone."

"Thomas, don't do this — let me come with you — " Gunter pleaded.

"Gunter, I need you here. I need you to watch over the pack. We don't know if the Nightstalkers are going to return for us. For me."

Gunter exhaled through his nostrils and softened his eyes. "As you wish, Thomas."

"Thank you. I'll be back." He gave Gunter a kiss and left the room. He glanced behind him at the two men he didn't think he could live without, telling himself he'd see them again.

\* \* \* \*

Thomas looked out beyond the trees and into Lake Michigan, breathing in the beauty before him. The Upper Peninsula truly was a calming place. Life was slower here. When one could be anything, anywhere was special. But this place was something unique.

The pier filled with boats coming and going. Horns blared and birds twittered above him. People near the docks laughed and swam and hugged each other. He thought he might not see this kind of peace for a long while.

And what he was here for was not the road to peace. He shifted from a bird back into himself, and dropped down from the tree, landing on his heels. He reached for his backpack, filled with clothes and snacks and water. He rested underneath the tree, closing his eyes and listening to the distant calls of the people on the pier. He was far enough away that they wouldn't spot him, in their little human bubbles, with small problems and even smaller worries. He wished he had that life. A simple life.

*But you did have that, and it was boring as hell, and lonely. And dark. But now…now your life has purpose. More purpose than you could have ever asked for. Nothing is more imperative right now than to protect your pack.*

He was uncomfortable being two hours away from Bramwell, but this needed to be done. *For André.*

The trees above him opened up in the breeze to let more sun in, the birds flitting around in a circle.

The future looked grim. And he didn't know what that meant for him and the pack. He feared for their futures, for his future, for Gunter's future. For their future together.

He didn't regret banishing Rhyse from the pack, but he did regret getting rid of a valuable asset. He hoped this Archimedes pack had someone with a similar skillset.

Then—

"Hey."

It startled him. He stood up and near him was a young man with gangly arms, beautiful ebony skin and an afro worthy of some kind of award. *Damn, that's a nice afro.*

Thomas was suddenly embarrassed to be naked.

"Oh—sorry, I—" he stammered, reaching for his bag.

"No, no, don't worry at all," the man said. "I'm from the Archimedes pack. We've been awaiting your arrival."

"How did you—?"

"See you coming? We have a Foresight."

"A Foresight?"

The man smiled. "Yeah, like your Rhyse. The fortune teller."

"Right. Well, he's out of the picture now."

"We know."

"So you have one, too? I mean, there are others?"

He laughed. "Of course there are more. Shit, there are more like you, aren't there?"

"Are there more like me in your pack?" Thomas asked eagerly.

The man smiled again. "I'm Dax. You should follow me."

So Thomas followed this stranger into the belly of the forest. He glanced back at the pier, not sure when he'd find that kind of peace again.

# Want to see more like this?
## Here's a taster for you to enjoy!

# Bound to the Spirits:
# Rattling Chains
## T. Strange

### *Excerpt*

Harlan stared at the scuffed, dented metal strip across the bottom of the doorway. Behind him was worn linoleum, with a pattern so familiar that he could have drawn it from memory. Ahead was a concrete sidewalk. It was scribbled with cracks, and there were piles of sodden leaves gathered anywhere the wind couldn't touch them, dark spots where people had spat out their gum, cigarette butts, candy wrappers and so many *people*.

Inside — order, sameness, routine.

Outside — chaos, change… Excitement.

Harlan wasn't looking for excitement or change. He wanted very much to turn around, away from the physical and mental threshold the doorway represented and vanish into the building that had housed him since he had been five years old.

"Do you need a push?" Tom asked, gently.

It was still difficult for Harlan to think of him as Tom. He'd known the man since he was eight as 'Mr. Addison'.

Mr. Addison had called Harlan into his office a few days before. There had been a paper on his desk with an official-looking stamp that Harlan hadn't been able to identify before the man had covered it with his broad, hairy hand.

'Am...am I in trouble, Mr. Addison?'

Mr. Addison had laughed and said, 'No, of course not! Please, call me Tom. You're an adult now, and I'm no longer your teacher.'

Those words had dropped something heavy and poisonous deep into Harlan's guts and it had stayed there for the last three days. It had been there while he'd packed his few belongings, while he'd said goodbye to everyone he'd ever known his whole life — everyone who gave any kind of shit about him, anyway.

Harlan shook his head. No, he didn't need — didn't *want* — a push. He wanted that letter to have never arrived. He wanted to stay in the Centre, the only home he could really remember.

After leaving him there, his parents had visited for a few years, and it had been strained for all three of them. Then Harlan's parents had had a new baby, one without 'the' ability. They'd visited once a month, then twice a year — his birthday and Christmas — then just sent cards. And after a few years...nothing. He couldn't remember the last time he'd heard from them, but it wasn't a relationship he intended to pursue, in or out of the Centre. They'd made it clear that they wanted nothing to do with him — and the feeling was mutual.

He didn't really consider anyone at the Centre his family, but it was his home, and he was being forced to leave with only his tiny, overstuffed duffle bag. Most of the things inside were just silly little presents the other kids had made him, not even personal items. He was also holding an envelope that Mr. Addison — Tom — had pressed into his hand with great importance, telling him there was three thousand dollars in it.

Harlan had never had to worry about money before. The resident children were given allowances, to spend or save as they chose, and some kids snuck out of the Centre to buy candy — or cigarettes and alcohol when they were older — but Harlan had never been tempted to leave. He'd been given everything he needed there, and they'd kept him safe. A cigarette that smelled bad and made him cough or a beer that made his head swim and made him sick in the morning weren't worth the risk of stepping beyond the Centre's encircling walls. He would have been happy to stay forever, maybe even eventually become a teacher like Mr. Addison... Tom. But apparently that wasn't his decision to make.

"Harlan? Is everything all right?" Tom asked.

No. Everything was *not* all right. It would never be all right again. "Fine, Mr. — *Tom.*"

Tom grinned at Harlan — the smile of a man who would, in just a few minutes, be shutting himself back in the safety of the Centre, closing out the rest of the world.

Harlan tried to return the smile, close-mouthed, afraid that if he opened it, he'd throw up.

Looking past Harlan, Tom waved. "Ah! Your ride's here!"

A sleek, black car with tinted windows drew up beside them. The driver climbed out, circled the car and opened the door closest to Harlan without speaking.

"You've got everything?" Tom asked. The too-enthusiastic, bubbly voice that had encouraged Harlan as an eight-year-old didn't have the same effect at twenty-one.

Harlan shrugged, throwing his bag into the back seat and climbing in after it.

Tom sprawled one elbow on the roof of the car, leaning way down until his face was uncomfortably close to Harlan's. "Great! And don't worry — the car's been specially treated. Didn't want to stress you out too much on your first day! Give me a call if you need *anything*." His voice was positively saccharine, and Harlan wanted to punch it.

Tom slammed the door and rapped on the trunk as though he were dismissing an ambulance.

Harlan didn't look back.

He closed his eyes when he saw the first ghost. He'd seen plenty, first as a kid, then when his parents finally realized what was going on, in the controlled environment of the Centre. As a child, he hadn't understood that other people couldn't see his 'visitors.' They'd been excellent playmates, until one *wouldn't* go away. Harlan had been too afraid to sleep, jumping at noises no one else could hear, having screaming fits with no apparent cause.

His parents had taken him to psychiatrist after psychiatrist, desperate to deny that their son might be a medium. They'd wanted something medical, something they could cure with pills and therapy. They hadn't wanted their son to be one of *those* people.

Answering the doctors' questions, Harlan realized for the first time that he really was the only one who saw the 'see-through people'. He'd always thought his parents were just ignoring them.

The psychiatrists tried to convince Harlan — and his parents — that it was just a phase, imaginary, nothing to be afraid of. The ghosts didn't go away, no matter how hard Harlan tried not to believe in them. Finally, the Centre had called Harlan's folks. He'd found out later that one of the psychiatrists they'd seen had taken pity on Harlan, contacted the Centre and informed them she had a patient who was potentially a medium. The Centre had invited Harlan and his parents for a tour. His mom and dad certainly didn't *believe* in that sort of thing, despite the overwhelming scientific evidence, but they had run out of options and Harlan wouldn't even go into his bedroom without screaming. He hadn't slept in days, and the whole family had been desperate.

Young as he'd been, Harlan remembered his first step past the threshold of the Centre. It was...silent. There were no voices here — unlike everywhere else, where they surrounded him like a wall of sound, people he could and couldn't see clamouring for his attention. There was no one but those he knew were really there — him and his parents. He realized he'd never felt this blissfully alone before. There had *always* been ghosts. And now they were gone.

He closed his eyes and breathed it in — the silence, the solitude.

He startled when he felt a soft touch on his shoulder. A few minutes of peace had been wonderful, but he knew it couldn't last.

An older man — even older than the grandparents Harlan was no longer allowed to see after he'd frightened them by passing on messages from people who'd died long before he was born — was kneeling in front of him.

"You must be Harlan."

Not wanting to speak, to shatter this beautiful silence, Harlan nodded.

The man smiled. "Do you like it here, Harlan?"

"Yes! Very much!" Harlan had said. He'd been afraid that if he didn't speak up, didn't answer this man's question, he might have to leave. He'd wanted to stay...as long as possible. Just a few more minutes.

"There's someone I'd like you to meet. If I'm right, she won't be much of a surprise to you. And if I'm wrong, you can go on home."

Harlan nodded again, fighting to keep his face blank. He didn't *want* to go home, where it was always noisy and crowded with people only he could see or hear, never mind the *thing* in his bedroom—

The man offered Harlan his hand to shake, just as seriously as he would an adult.

Harlan shook, just as solemnly. The man's hand was pleasantly cool and dry, and he didn't squeeze too hard. Harlan wished his own hands weren't so clammy.

"I'm Dr. Cunningham, the director here at the Centre. It's a pleasure to meet you, Harlan."

Harlan tensed—just another doctor, more tests to see what kind of crazy he was. And that was a pity, because it was so *lovely* here. Harlan didn't think he was crazy, but his parents did, so he must be. They just hadn't found anyone who could prove it.

Dr. Cunningham laughed. "Don't worry. I'm not... This test will be different than any you've done before. I promise."

Standing, Dr. Cunningham gave Harlan's parents a reassuring wave before immediately returning his attention to Harlan. "Would you like to come with me?"

Harlan had heard plenty of stories from ghosts about how to tell if someone was dangerous, what would get a person killed and who to trust. Dr. Cunningham felt safe and genuine.

He nodded, allowing Dr. Cunningham to take his hand and lead him deeper into the building. They left his parents behind, but he didn't mind very much.

This part of the building was different. The front part, where they'd come in and where they'd left Harlan's parents, had carpets and art on the walls, like a hotel lobby. Here, the floors were bare concrete, the walls plain white with pipes visible overhead.

Dr. Cunningham's shoes clicked as he walked. The sound, the way the doctor walked with confidence, as though he belonged here and expected everyone to know it, made Harlan feel special. He belonged here, too, and he'd take any test they wanted to prove it.

Maybe reading Harlan's excitement as nervousness, Dr. Cunningham gave his hand a gentle squeeze. "Don't worry. The dormitories are far more comfortable. This is the lab, and you won't be spending much time here. That is," he said, smiling down at Harlan, "if you pass this test, which I very much think you will."

The doctor winked, and again Harlan felt as though he was being included in a wonderful secret, one not even his parents knew.

"We have a ghost in here."

Harlan stiffened. He'd never had a grownup talk about a ghost like it was real, and he felt a surge of bitterness when he realized the doctor had just been making fun of him like everyone else did.

Dr. Cunningham gave Harlan a reassuring smile. "Don't worry. She's quite safe. She won't hurt you." He laughed. "She actually used to work here, in the lab. She always talked about becoming a research ghost when she died." His face turned grim. "She should have had many years ahead of her, but... Well, she still works here, just in a different capacity. You don't have to be afraid."

"I'm not afraid." He was, though—afraid that Dr. Cunningham was teasing him and afraid that he *wasn't*. Ever since that horrible woman had taken over his bedroom, ghosts weren't fun anymore.

"Good lad." Dr. Cunningham gave Harlan's shoulder a brief squeeze. "I'll be right here with you the whole time. When you're ready, step onto that pad." He pointed at a metal circle set in the concrete floor. "This whole building is warded against ghosts, except for a few select places like that one. You won't run into any by accident here…if you choose to stay."

Harlan bit his lower lip, hard, so he wouldn't cry. He wanted to stay. He *had* to pass this test.

"If, at any time, you get scared or you want to stop, just step outside the circle and she'll disappear again."

"W-what do I have to do?"

"Just talk to her. Say 'hi'. It's only polite. She'll tell you a special word that will let me know you've really seen her."

"I just have to talk?"

Dr. Cunningham nodded.

Harlan drew in a slow, deep breath and briefly closed his eyes. He could do that. He'd always found it easier to talk to ghosts than to 'real' people. He could never tell what the living were thinking or feeling, but ghosts kind of…projected their feelings, whether they meant to or not.

Breath hitching in his chest, Harlan stepped forward onto the pad. He realized he had his eyes closed and had to force them open. His hands were trembling.

She appeared slowly, not just popping into his view the way ghosts sometimes did, and he suspected she'd done it on purpose so she wouldn't scare him.

"Hello. Are you Harlan?"

He nodded, just a tiny tilt of his head. He'd learned to hide when he was listening to a ghost, and he almost never spoke to them out loud anymore. He glanced back at Dr. Cunningham, but he just gave Harlan an encouraging nod. He didn't look at all angry or mocking.

"It's very nice to meet you. I'm Gwen. Are you ready for the word?"

He nodded again, a little more confidently.

"The word is 'ludicrous'. Ludicrous. You'll remember?"

"Yes," he said, shyly.

She waved and started slowly fading.

He stepped out of the circle and turned to face Dr. Cunningham again. "She said…ludicrous."

Dr. Cunningham beamed. "You passed the test."

# About the Author

Kegan was born in Pennsylvania in 1993. He has always been a creative—at the age of 8 he created a comic book series, and he wrote his first novel at age 14. His love of vampires and werewolves paired with his love of gay erotica resulted in his passion project, The Blood Crusades.

He enjoys pop music, horror flicks, Halloween, science fiction, the works of Stephen King, and video games. In his writing, he strives to represent LGBTQIA+ individuals. You'll find his works chock-full of LGBTQIA+ characters living their lives passionately and with conviction.

He lives in Wisconsin.

Kegan loves to hear from readers. You can find his contact information, website details and author profile page at https://www.pride-publishing.com

PUBLISHING

Sign up for our newsletter and find out about all our romance book releases, eBook sales and promotions, sneak peeks and FREE romance books!